WITH THIS WISH

Windswept Bay, Book Nine

DEBRA CLOPTON

CHAPTER ONE

The wind blew hot and humid across Trent Sinclair as he rode his Harley along the curving shoreline road of Windswept Bay. He had been rebuilding this vintage Knucklehead Harley for two years and now it purred like a big kitten. Knowing he'd rebuilt it with his own hands was a rewarding feeling. It gave him a sense of accomplishment.

It had also kept him busy in the evenings.

Kept his mind busy and he needed that after he'd been released from the military and special ops. He hadn't managed well when he first came home almost three years ago and finding the bike several months after arriving had been a lifeline that he'd needed. He hadn't wanted to hang out, or go out at all. Other than seeing his family—his brothers and sisters—most of the time after he finished work, he'd just wanted time alone. But he'd found too much time spent with nothing but the sound of crickets, frogs, and even the sound of the small waterfall not too far away through the trees didn't work well for him… It enabled too much time for memories, regrets, and stagnation.

He'd realized he needed something to help him mark time and working on the Harley had been exactly the right project. But now it was finished. And time had moved on, life had moved on… But was he ready?

Had his heart healed enough? Did he want to reach for more?

There was no hurry. Now, he'd take pleasure in this—riding, feeling the life that vibrated in the air as he rode the Harley. For now, that was what he'd focus on. That and taking one step at a time toward moving forward at last.

He studied the surf as he followed the curve of the

road and thought how lucky he was to live in such a beautiful spot. He turned onto the secluded road that led up the hillside and away from the blue waters of the bay. He enjoyed the seclusion of his tree-surrounded home away from the surf, contrary to what most people wanted out of a home near the beach. As he wound up the hill and rounded the last curve to his driveway, he had to yank the bike hard to the left to miss the baby-blue travel trailer blocking the road.

The bike skidded and he managed to miss a tree as he careened through the ditch, caught air and skidded to a halt in his driveway. He cut the ignition and dropped the kickstand to the Knucklehead.

Who... What?

The questions blasted through him as he glared toward the faded Chevy attached to the small egg-shaped travel trailer that blocked his drive and the road. Anger flashed through him as he scanned the area, no one was there.

"Are you all right?"

He yanked his head around and saw a blonde standing halfway between him and the house, a look of shock on her tanned face. What little he could see of her face for the mass of hair.

"What are you thinking?" he demanded as he hauled off the bike and strode toward her. "You trying to get someone killed with that rig of yours?"

"No. I thought it was off the road enough. I have my flashers on."

"Nope, no flashers and not off the road enough."

She pushed curls from her face with one hand and left her hand on her forehead, as if to hold the mass back. Her brow wrinkled above her dark shades. "Well, I'll move it. I was under the impression there was little traffic from here on up the hillside."

"True enough, but still not a good thing. You should have moved it at least out of the way of the curve and my driveway."

"Fine. I'll move it and be right back." She jogged past him in an easy stride.

He set his hands on his hips and watched as she yanked open the passenger door, slid inside, and then yanked it closed. She scooted to the driver's seat and gunned the engine. A loud backfire boomed from the old truck before it lunged forward and towed the blue egg across his driveway and up the road ten feet past the entrance of his home. That was one ugly little trailer.

But one really cute owner, he noticed as within moments, she was jogging back his way. Her hair seemed alive as she loped up his asphalt and stopped in front of him. She pulled her shades off, exposing her pretty, makeup-less skin and sparkling eyes the color of periwinkles that grew in his mother's window boxes. She let her hand holding the shades drop to her thigh and his gaze followed the movement, past her T-shirt with Yosemite National Park scrawled across her small breasts, to a pair of cutoff jeans that hit just above mid-thigh on her tanned, well-toned legs. His gaze snagged on the shades as she tapped them on the side of her thigh near the long, jagged scar that ran down the side of her left leg. The scar had been hidden from his view as she'd jogged past on her way to the truck but now, though faded, it was an obvious leftover from what he envisioned as a painful accident or surgery.

"So, now that I have that out of the way, we can talk."

Her happy voice had him yanking his gaze off her legs back to meet her clear gaze. She smiled and instantly went from pretty to knockout in one swift kick in the gut.

"Talk?" he muttered, struggling to pull his attention from the pain of her injury to the happy lilt of her tone and those eyes. *That smile. It was completely disconcerting.*

"Yes, first, I love your ride. A real beauty." She turned to look at the Knucklehead and his gaze snagged again on the vicious scar. It was faded but from this angle clearly had once, years ago, been terrible.

Trent's thoughts went back momentarily to a time he tried hard not to remember. He shook his head and forced his attention to his Harley. "Thanks. I like it."

She turned back, her smile wide. "I hope you'll give me a ride at some point. I can only imagine the freedom of it. And I'm sure it purrs smooth as butter as you ride."

His concentration faltered at her words. "You know vintage bikes?" As startling as every second since he'd come up on her was the instant attraction that shot through him. His mind faltered because it had been awhile since he'd been instantly attracted to someone…not since Erica. Thinking of Erica, he forced himself to focus on the intriguing woman. On finding out who she was and why she was here.

"I don't really know them. I've just been around a lot of motorcycles and a vintage bike stands out." Lilly McCall took in the gorgeous guy in front of her. He stood out, too, more than his motorcycle. He was tall, lean and hard muscle and though she'd done her research on him before, she hadn't been prepared for the unexpected attraction buzzing through her. That could be a problem. "I'm Lilly McCall," she said, realizing she'd never introduced herself.

"I'm Trent Sinclair, but I have a feeling you already know that." His head cocked. "McCall. Wait, are you my brother-in-law BJ's sister?"

She nodded. "I am. But he has no idea I'm here yet." She extended her hand and she saw her reflection in his aviators and could see her crazy hair was pretty wild from the salt air and the fact that she'd been riding with the windows open for the last four hours. She was a bit of a mess with it having expanded to twice its normal size. *Oh well, it was what it was.*

He took her hand and shook in a firm, professional manner. She liked the feel of his callused palm though it was a very brief handshake. "Are you lost?"

She smiled. "No, I know exactly where I'm at."

He removed his aviators and her heart skipped a beat as striking blue eyes the color of the teal-toned water of the coast met hers.

"So, you came to see me?" His gaze locked onto hers, probing.

Awareness churned in her chest and she fought it off like a woman fighting off bees. The man was as sexy as the heroes of the books she wrote and she couldn't have written a heroine's reaction any better than her reaction to him.

"Well, in part but I'm also on my way to my

place."

He crossed his arms—his distractingly muscled arms—and his brows dipped. "Your place?"

She was confusing him. She did tend to do that. *Focus, Lilly.* "I'm here about a treehouse. I want you to build me one."

He hitched an eyebrow. "You know about my treehouses?"

"I do. I was talking to BJ a month ago and he was telling me what each of his new brothers-in-law do. And he mentioned that you'd been building treehouses. And, well, I started thinking about it and couldn't let the idea go. So, here I am and I'd like you to build me one. If you have time. And I'm really hoping you do." She really did. She was set on it, actually. This move she was making was huge for her. Deciding to take hold of her life and set down roots. It was big. It was hard and the whimsical idea of living in a treehouse had taken hold of her like a vise and wouldn't let go. She wanted this treehouse. *Truly wanted to plant roots and stay...*

"Where? Don't you travel around a lot? Like from

one national park to the other or something like that?"

Her heart tugged. "I do. I mean, I did. I'm starting a new chapter in my life, though. I'm..." She moistened her lips and the soles of her feet suddenly itched. "I'm settling down. Here on Windswept Bay. BJ is here."

"Well, I think that's great. He didn't mention you were coming last time I talked to him."

"He doesn't know."

Trent looked shocked now. "Really, you're surprising him?"

"Yes, I am." She hadn't wanted anyone to know her plan. She'd made it, was used to making decisions on her own and flying by the seat of her pants. "I'm going to see him but I wanted to settle in first and get things with the treehouse rolling."

"Rolling?"

"Yes. Can you fit a treehouse into your schedule over the next few months?"

He placed his hands on his jean-clad hips and studied her with real consternation now. "Well, I am finishing up a remodel in a couple of days but I have another job scheduled in two months."

"Great. That's plenty of time, isn't it?"

He laughed. "Maybe. Depends on how extravagant you want it."

"Nice, but not extravagant. I'm not an extravagant kind of person."

"Okay, so where is the spot? I'll need to look at it."

"Fantastic. It's just around the corner, up the hill."

He blinked. "This hill?"

She nodded as if she hadn't said anything startling, but she had. "Yes, up the road."

"*You* bought the property at the top of this hill?"

Lilly shouldn't have been surprised by his reaction. Of course he would know what the property at the top of this hill would cost. He lived right here mid-way up the road to it.

"I did." And his reaction was right, the property hadn't come cheap. She wondered what was going through his mind. Probably thought she had a loan from BJ. The truth was far from that. "Look, I'll pay whatever you want, if that's what's worrying you. But I do have a deadline. I need it within the next two months."

"Okay, but you're sure you want a treehouse up *there*? This is the Florida coast and we do have hurricanes from time to time."

"I'm sure. I'll deal with the hurricanes when they come. But I know what I want. Can you do it? I've checked out your work and love it." She placed her hands on her hips and prepared herself to convince him to do this, no matter what it took. "I know what I want and you can give that to me."

His brow rose and the suggestive connotation of her words slammed into her. Being a twenty-six-year-old phenomenon who hid inside her volunteer work inside the national park service slightly hindered her love life. And there was the fact that a knot lived inside her that couldn't—wouldn't—loosen its hold on her heart. She could write her quirky, sweet romances but to actually open up to them herself was something she didn't think she would ever be able to do.

So she just wrote love stories…there was no threat of pain if she let that be enough. Truth was, there had never been any attraction toward someone who challenged her heart.

He was staring at her and she realized he'd never answered. "Look, are you the man for the job?"

His lips twitched and his eyes crinkled at the edges. "I might be. I'll have to take a look at the property first. Maybe we should drive up there and take a look at what exactly you want in this slightly restrictive scenario you've just described."

She laughed with relief. She had him and she knew it. "Great! Let's go. Your ride or mine?"

CHAPTER TWO

Trent laughed at the way she smiled and teased about riding his Harley. He wasn't sure what to make of Lilly McCall. And the fact that she'd come here before going to see her brother seemed off. But then, BJ had said that he and his sister had both been wanderers after they'd lost their parents. Not that they'd talked a lot about it. His brother-in-law didn't talk a lot about his past. Trent just knew that his parents and Lilly had been in a car wreck and that Lilly had lived and they hadn't. It had been a bad time in their life. Trent understood about not wanting to talk about something that cut so deep. He'd had his own tragedy…had his own way of coping. Olivia knew more about BJ's past but hadn't said much either, just that he hoped one day Lilly would feel able to open up to being close to family again. Olivia had helped BJ do that.

Looking at Lilly now, Trent couldn't help wondering whether this was Lilly taking that major step toward healing. He had slowly let his family back into his life—not completely—there was just too much pain in his heart from losing Erica so tragically, so suddenly that he didn't think he could ever completely share that with anyone. But he lived among his family and there had been no closing them out completely, no getting away from the fact that if something happened to one of them, a person he loved, that he would hurt. Pain, love, joy and loss were all intertwined like balls of thread and one way or another could not completely be disconnected. Still, some tried. He wondered whether that was what Lilly had done.

"Hey, I was just teasing. I'll take my truck and move the trailer out of the way."

He realized he'd not said anything as she'd backed toward his bike. He'd just stood there like a dope, watching her and thinking. "Okay, I'll follow you," he offered.

She gave him a thumbs-up and then turned and jogged up the incline to her truck. He was getting on his Knucklehead when her truck revved to life, backfired and then lurched forward.

That thing had a problem. Obviously needed a tune-up.

As he followed her, he couldn't help thinking she had paid a pretty sum for the lot at the top of the hill. And she'd said she'd pay whatever the cost was for the treehouse. She acted as if money was no object. Then again, BJ was worth a bundle. Had inherited it from his long-lost dad and was still adjusting to that fact, so maybe he'd shared it with his sister. BJ's background was complicated.

But either he'd shared some of his newfound wealth with his sister or the lady was loaded on her own, because the hilltop hadn't come cheap. Trent's grandfather had owned the lot he'd built his home on but it was not the top of the hill. The lot with the view. A price tag to match.

She had bought it.

He followed her up the winding road, dappled by the sun peeking through the trees. When they reached the gate, she drove on through.

The land wasn't on the beach but it was optimal property and access wasn't that easy. Yes, it had a paved road to an extent and then there was a lot of vegetation that would require clearing, at least part of the way. And then depending on what kind of treehouse she was looking for... He had done regular, no-nonsense but unique treehouses that weren't extravagant but still, plumbing and water access and security didn't come cheap. And then he had done extravagant treehouses that were gorgeous and completely unique. He had a feeling—well, to be honest, he didn't have a feeling; he had no idea what she wanted. He would just wait and see. It hit him suddenly that she must have come to town at some point to shop for the property.

He pulled up behind her and the blue egg travel

trailer that she pulled up beside the small cabin on the property. She climbed out and hurried toward him as he cut the engine and got off his bike.

She was smiling brightly. "I can't wait to show you my tree. Have to find it first. I'm so excited at the thought of getting my treehouse."

He paused. "Did you come visit BJ at some point and find this property?"

She raked her hand through her curls, pushing it back out of its ever-present attempt to get into her eyes. "I found it on the Internet for sale and then I looked it up on Google Maps and zeroed in on it."

"You picked out a tree over the Internet?"

"Well, I think so. At least it looks pretty tall when I zoom in on it. You'll have to help me find it, since I haven't actually seen it in real life."

She'd googled her tree. He tried not to let his disbelief show in his expression. He was glad he'd put his aviators back on to hide his eyes. He turned to stare at the mass of trees surrounding them. "Any idea which direction?"

She glanced at the cabin and then turned north and

walked away from it across the barely there road and looked into the woods and then up. "It's in there." She moved into the trees. She wore sturdy hiking boots.

He watched her go. She had the stride of a woman comfortable moving around in dense trees. It hit him then that she'd worked most of the last several years in national parks. She would naturally be comfortable among trees. He followed her, more than curious to see her tree. *Her Google Mapped tree.*

"There it is!" Delight was in her squeal as she pointed upward and he knew exactly which one she pointed to considering it peaked up above the tops of the other trees. She had started forward again and he followed.

They had to go slow because there was a lot of underbrush but finally they reached the tree.

"It's beautiful. Don't you love it? I can't wait to write here. I mean, I have the little cabin for now, which will feel like a palace compared to my little trailer but I can't wait to live and write in my treehouse. I want open space, windows, and well, I'm open to your creative ideas." She spun toward him.

Excitement illuminated her expression. "What do you think?"

Think? You're beautiful. He was startled by how right she looked here among the trees, earthy and vibrant with her wild hair and easy manner.

"Will it work for a treehouse?" she asked when he'd said nothing.

What was wrong with him? He wasn't used to being off-centered by a woman but that was exactly how he felt looking at Lilly. "It'll work." He yanked his gaze off her and stared at her tree. It was perfect, with thick, strong limbs to build around. Studying it, his imagination began to whirl. "You had a good eye, even looking down with a satellite view. I'm still amazed by that."

She laughed. "They are fairly detailed. And I was taking a bit of a chance but I talked to the Realtor, too, and she assured me that the property had a lot of strong trees. She was probably curious about why I was so interested in the trees but I didn't tell her my plans."

He moved forward to get a closer look. "It will do nicely."

"Awesome. I can see myself up there writing. Creating."

He studied her now. "So you're a writer? BJ or my sister never mentioned that."

She cocked her head to the side. "That's because they don't know."

That startled him. "They don't know?" She shrugged when he was certain she read the surprise in his expression.

"I write under a pen name. Chloe Beck. Have been for several years now."

He would not have pictured her as a writer; then again, he'd never really known a writer so he wasn't really sure why he couldn't picture her as one. "So, let me get this straight. BJ, your brother, doesn't know you've come to town, bought property, are building a treehouse or that you're a writer?"

She looked suddenly a little torn. "True to all of the above. It's complicated."

"Sounds like it."

"I'm going to tell him tomorrow. I just needed…" She paused and for the first time since he'd met her, she looked vulnerable, uncertain. Then she blinked it away and gave him a quick smile. "I needed to get myself set up on my own. You'll learn I'm pretty much a loner. I can't help it. BJ knows it. Understands it."

"Sure. I was just asking." It wasn't his business anyway. It wasn't like him to pry. He kept to himself too. "I've heard a lot of writers use fake names."

"Pen names. For various reasons. For a while there, I tried to hide it but the truth is that I love what I do and am very good at it. But I like my anonymity."

It was obvious that she wasn't trying to impress anyone considering she drove a faded truck, lived in an old trailer and wore cutoff shorts. "I get it. I like hiding out in the trees myself."

She smiled widely. "Two peas in a pod. So, when can you start?" She swung back to her tree and he focused his attention off looking at her to the tree.

He laughed; he couldn't help it. "Maybe so. So, what kind of books do you write?"

"I write romantic love stories. Sweet ones, the kind you would see on the Hallmark Channel. Not particularly something that would appeal to a guy like you."

He crossed his arms. "So how do you know I don't like Hallmark movies?"

She laughed and shot him a sideways glance. "Do you? I have a lot of male readers. I just didn't picture you as the romantic type."

"Wow, you've put me in a nice, neat box."

"Sorry, I just assumed…"

"Why would I not like a good love story?"

"Maybe I jumped the gun. Do you have a girlfriend?"

"No, I don't have a girlfriend. I haven't been looking for one in a while."

"Me too. I don't date."

"Why did you ask?" His head spun from the way she moved from one conversation to the next. It had been a long time since he had even been interested. After losing Erica, after all that had been taken from him physically and emotionally, he just needed time to himself. But lately he'd been restless and for the first time since that terrible day Erica had been killed, he felt a stir of interest toward Lilly, even with the way she made his head spin.

Whether it would go any further than that was yet to be seen. If he took this job on nothing would happen, because he never crossed business with personal. He was still curious about why she'd asked if he had a girlfriend.

"I don't know, actually. My luck with men is not that great. Besides, my working schedule is crowded. Full throttle, hectic. I have deadlines I set that I need to meet. And it helps me not think about the dating thing."

"This conversation is getting more curious by the minute. The dating *thing*?"

"Well, you know, the whole conflict that comes with dating. Distraction. The drama. All that I don't have time for right now. So, the dating *thing*—too complicated. I write about it but have no want for it in my own life."

He stared at her, a little dumbfounded. "Are you worried about me asking you out? Or hitting on you? Because you don't have to worry about that. If I take this job, there'll be no 'thing' between us. I'll be working for you. So you can rest easy, hole up all you want, and I'll go about my business and do what you've hired me to do. How does that sound?"

She stared at him as if he had just sprouted a second head. "Oh, I wasn't saying that to imply you were going to hit on me or ask me out. Sorry, I stick my foot in my mouth more times than not. That's another reason me and working in the deep woods has always worked. I get along well with wildlife. They listen to me talk and never misunderstand. I was just saying that to say that me being up here is going to be perfect. Secluded, but my own private place. I've been cramped inside my little blue trailer there for years among the other workers. But I actually stopped working for the park service a year ago and have been renting a spot at a camping site and writing. Still, it wasn't like my own place. And well, I finally told BJ I was going to settle down soon. I just haven't told him everything. I wanted to get everything figured out before I told anyone. I need this to be my doing." She stopped her rapid fire deluge and took a deep breath.

He was lost. Really lost. She was cute, but as far

as he was concerned, *she* was complicated—without getting into all her reasons for not wanting a complicated life. It sounded as if she had a little bit of a…he didn't really know how to put it but it was something.

"Why don't you tell me what you want in this treehouse of yours?" He needed to get them back on the business end of this. She might have interested him, but he already had red flags flying up everywhere. Lilly McCall was obviously more complicated than anything he was interested in.

CHAPTER THREE

Lilly's motor mouth had gotten her in trouble once more. *Why did she always do that?* She always rattled off more than she meant to say. Especially if she was nervous. And the macho—Mr. Romance Novel Hero Man—made her nervous. She wanted him to build this treehouse for her. *So why had she told him all her personal stuff? It was ridiculous.* Sometimes she just wanted to slap a hand over her mouth or stuff tissues in it so she would keep quiet. *But*, she sighed, *she only told him the truth. Just too much.*

Sometimes she wrote for days and days.

Sometimes she forgot to bathe—yes, yuck but true. *Sometimes* she was so into her stories that she didn't want anybody to disturb her. And most of the time she was a mess.

What guy would want that?

What guy could put up with that?

None. Nope, it would be asking for too much.

Trent was quietly studying her, waiting.

Waiting on an answer about your treehouse plans, silly. Lilly gasped. "Plans! I want you to help me come up with them. I know that I need to get at least one room at the top where I can see the ocean. Do you think I could see the ocean from up there?" She squinted upward at the tall tree. "I like being in the trees, like the seclusion of it, but I'd really like to see the ocean while I'm creating—I think it would be wonderful and something I've never had before. And then openness downstairs and room for a bed. It doesn't have to be gigantic; it just needs to be sturdy and nice. And unique. To tell you the truth, I'm going to start a new series and I want to write that series in the treehouse. My new series, and don't tell anyone, my heroine in the story—she's a cozy detective. And she lives in a treehouse. And I want to feel that while I'm creating her stories. I want to be able to do this series from my own treehouse. I think it will be unique and I think it will be something my readers will enjoy knowing as behind-the-scenes info on the series. It's really appealing to me. But I need your expertise to get me there. Does that get your creative ideas flowing? Do you think you can do that? Can you help me?"

A wide smile took over his face and he raised his aviators up to stare at her with those gorgeous ocean blues. He looked a little dazed. She was used to people looking at her that way. Dazed and confused. Which she sometimes felt herself, but she really thought in whirlwinds sometimes and couldn't help herself. She grimaced. "Did I lose you?"

He chuckled. "I'll tell *you* the truth, I'm going to take this job. And one reason is because you intrigue the dickens out of me. I'm not real sure if your mind works faster than your mouth, but I want to do this project just to find out where it goes." He laughed, and his eyes twinkled. "And Olivia would probably kill me if I didn't take the job for her new sister-in-law. I promise I'll let you write and I'll get my job done so you can create this character of yours up in your treehouse."

"*Yes!* And you can do it in two months?"

"I can do it within two months if we get going quickly. I have a job starting after that and so it will actually work into my schedule. However, we'll need to come up with the idea and stick with it pretty close. You won't be able to start changing your mind all over the place. Can you do that? Not change things up every few days?"

Despite his skeptical question, she wanted to hug him. "I can do that. Really, I can. Let's design it. I want to see your ideas and then I'll let you do your thing while I do mine. I have to finish up the deadline I'm on right now so I'll stay out of your hair. We will both be busy. It's perfect. I'll have to see BJ and Olivia, too, some."

"I have a feeling you're going to see them some. They'll know where to find you." He took out his phone and started snapping pictures of the tree.

She watched him snapping lots of pictures and followed him as he moved. "Yes, you're right. But I'll have to make sure they know I need my alone time."

He glanced at her and she halted before she slammed into him. She was suddenly worried about protecting her writing time. She'd come here to force herself to start getting involved with people again. She'd drifted further and further away from people over the last year. And even she had recognized that that wasn't healthy. But this was going to take some getting used to. But it would work out. She looked up at her tree and breathed in a fortifying breath.

"This is going to be good. Perfect." She shot Trent a smile then stared at her tree again. *Better than perfect...*

As he followed Lilly back to the small cabin, he decided, just from knowing her the short time that he had, that there was no way she would be able to stay on target and budget. With the way she skipped around from one topic to the other, he could see the nightmare of the next couple of months. One minute, she'd want the kitchen on the north side of the treehouse; the next instant, she'd want it reversed. It would be one headache after the other. He should say he couldn't do it. He should walk away.

But he wouldn't. He knew how much Olivia and BJ had wanted Lilly to come here and try to settle down. If he didn't do what he could to help keep her here, then they would be upset. Oh, they'd get over it. But there was no way he'd let them down. Besides that, something told him that deep down, Lilly needed to be here. She might not know it but he felt it was true.

His only hope was that she held her almighty deadline in as high regard as it seemed she did. If that were so, then maybe between her holing up and working on it and getting to know her family again, she would leave him alone and let him get the work done.

That was what he was counting on. Her very tight schedule.

"Do you have time to discuss the plans? Or do you

have time to get to it tonight? The sooner the better."

She didn't waste time. "Look, it's dinnertime and you've got to be tired from driving. What if we go down the road to the Shrimp Shack—you passed it on the way here. We can eat on the deck, relax and discuss plans. I'll bring my sketchpad and get details started. Strictly business."

"I am a little hungry. I can get settled in here tomorrow so let's go."

"You're going to stay here tonight? I'm sure BJ and Olivia would welcome you to stay with them."

"No, I'll be staying in my trailer tonight and get settled into the cabin tomorrow."

He didn't push. "Okay, then if you want, hop on my bike and we'll head that way. We can get my truck at my house—"

"Or not. I want to ride this," she said, looking at him in surprise. "No need for the truck on my account."

"You're sure?"

"Oh yeah, you bet I am." She strode to the Harley and flourished a hand toward the bike. "After you."

He grinned and threw a leg over, let it off its stand and waited for her to settle in behind him. He wasn't prepared for the way his adrenaline jerked when she slipped her arms around his waist and held on. Warmth curled in the pit of his stomach and his pulse raced.

"Hold on," he warned and then they shot out of the driveway and down the winding road.

All the while, his heart thundered from the feel of her soft form pressed to his back.

Complicated?

This had complicated written all over it.

The Shrimp Shack was truly a shack of a place right on the beach.

"It's not much to look at but the shrimp is fresh and the best you'll find."

"Great." Lilly glanced around at the brightly colored little joint, glad to have something to concentrate on rather than the fact that she had been far too appreciative of the man she'd had her arms around coming down the hillside. Every fiber of her body had been more than cheering the fact that she was pressed up against the man. It had been a ferocious mental battle to talk herself into letting go of the sexy builder—and she'd had to firmly remind herself that he was her brother's brother-in-law and there had to be some sort of taboo associated with mauling the man who was now kin to her through marriage.

The conflict of the whole situation had her mind churning with story ideas…it was a setup that she would have to explore. *In her books. Not in real life. Not with Trent.*

No matter how sexy the man was, she was not interested in opening up her life to any more pain and suffering. After all, she had come here to let herself get to know her brother again. And his wife. That right there was enough to open herself up to the possibility of suffering.

She'd already decided that she was going to do this. Try to force herself to connect again. But after the nightmare of losing her parents, this was a first. And there were no guarantees that she was going to be able to do it.

The treehouse was part of her plan to help root her to the idea. She'd always dreamed of living in a treehouse. Hopefully fulfilling that dream would help her stick.

She just didn't know whether her heart could do it. "What do you want?"

She sucked her lip on one side, trying to get a handle on how she could apply all the angst she was feeling right now into the story scene she was working on.

"Lilly, knock knock. Do you know what you want?"

She was startled when Trent touched her arm and only then did she realize he'd been talking to her. "Oh, sorry," she said, just as her stomach growled like a lion, causing the teenage girl behind the counter to grin. "I guess I'm so hungry my hearing is off."

Trent chuckled. "This is the place to fill it up and make it happy. Lisa here can sure help you out."

"I sure can. Just fire away when you're ready. Our po' boy sandwiches are amazing. And the shrimp baskets are a favorite too." The girl smiled briefly at

Lilly and then returned her adoring gaze to Trent. "You want your usual, Trent?"

Lilly glanced at him as he smiled back at Lisa. "I do. I'm a sucker for the po' boy."

Lisa nodded and batted her eyes. Lilly could practically hear the poor girl's heart pounding with love and adoration. *Who could blame her?*

"I'll have what he's having then. If he likes it that much, it must be good."

Lisa nodded. "You won't be disappointed. I'll turn this in and they'll bring it to you. Go ahead and grab your drinks over there."

"Thanks, Lisa. You do a great job."

"Thanks. I try. I love this job."

Lilly hid her smile. She had a feeling that because Trent lived close, he probably came in here often to eat and that was a job bonus the girl was obviously been thrilled about.

They grabbed sodas and Trent held open the door for her. She brushed by him and was immediately reminded by her pulse spiking that she was not oblivious to her contractor either.

"Trent! Hey bro, come over here," a good-looking guy called from a green picnic table by the railing. He had dark, short hair nearly covering one eye and a smile that she was certain could break hearts. He waved them over.

"Jake, what are you doing here?" Trent led the way over to where the guy sat.

He stood as they reached them and smiled at her. "Hi, I'm Jake. His brother. I do not believe I have had the pleasure of meeting you." He held out his hand. "I was just finishing up my shrimp basket and now I'm glad I ate slow."

"This is Lilly, BJ's sister." Trent grunted and sat down across from him and she did, too, as Jake sat back down.

"No kidding?"

A young man came out and set their baskets of food on the table in front of them and then headed back inside after telling them to holler if they needed anything else.

"So you're the long-lost sister who lives in the trees." He grinned.

"Yep, that's me." She laughed.

"More than you know." Trent slid her a wink.

She realized he was giving her the opportunity to talk for herself instead of saying more than she might. "I've just moved to town and bought the lot at the top of the hill there. In the trees."

He grinned. "I saw BJ earlier and he didn't say anything about you being in town."

"I haven't told him. I'm telling him tomorrow."

"He'll be surprised."

"Yes, I'm hoping you'll help me with that surprise and not mention it to him or Olivia."

"Sure. Your surprise is safe with me. Besides, I have an all-day dive set up tomorrow, so by the time I get back to town the secret will be out."

"Oh, you own the dive shop. BJ told me one of you did. I couldn't remember which one."

"That's me. I love it. Can't get any of my brothers to come into the business and help me out, though." He shot Trent a teasing glower and then looked from Trent to her with obvious speculation in his eyes. "So what brings you two to be hanging out together?"

"Trent's my neighbor and he's just agreed to build a treehouse for me."

"No kidding? You're building a treehouse up the hill from Trent?" Disbelief rang in his words.

She nodded. "It's going to be great." She picked up her sandwich and took a bite.

He gave a low whistle. "That, I will have to see. A treehouse up the big hill, cool."

Trent set his sandwich down and picked up a french fry. "We're going to do some drawings and see where she wants to go with it. I'm squeezing it in between jobs."

"Sounds like a plan. So are you giving up your work with the parks?"

"I actually gave it up already. I've been writing part-time for years and went all in a little over a year ago."

"Writing? What?"

"Like you would know," Trent said, and she heard the teasing in his voice.

"Hey, I read. I like John Grisham."

"I write romance. And I am about to start some

cozy mysteries. My characters aren't as calm, cool, and collected as John Grisham's characters are."

"If you bought the top of that hill, you obviously don't need them to be."

She smiled. "They do all right by me." She thought about that statement as she glanced out across the white sand to the blue water ebbing and flowing in timeless motion. Her books did more than all right, and she was still in shock about how people loved to read her stories. Even more shocking to her was that she could write about love since she'd closed her own heart off to love the night she'd lost her parents. That cold, horrible night that she'd realized just how much it hurt to love and lose.

That she could write about love in a way that touched people's hearts sometimes baffled her. But then, love in her books was make-believe. It was safe. And in her books, everything always worked out right.

In real life, that wasn't always so. And maybe that was why she was so good at what she did…pretending was far easier than the truth. Some people believed loving was worth the risk of losing.

She didn't. Not anymore. So she would stick to writing. Stick to creating stories that she controlled the endings to. Stick to writing happily-ever-afters that made her and her readers smile.

Yes, she'd come here to start a new life in Windswept Bay...to be closer to BJ, because she had finally reached a time that she was drawn to trying to open up, to being close again. But she was going to keep walls of protection around most of her heart. Walls that no one could penetrate.

"Well, I need to head out. Nice meeting you, tree girl." Jake shot her a wink that made her smile.

"Nice meeting you too. Come see the house any time."

"Will do. Later, Trent."

They watched him leave, striding off the deck and toward his truck.

"He's nice. Y'all don't look anything alike, though," she observed.

"He and his brother Max aren't our blood brothers. They were our best friends and when their parents died, they came to live with us. Later, Mom and Dad adopted them. We're all really close."

The fact that Jake and Max had lost their parents snagged her attention. "They lost their parents?"

"Yes. It was really a hard time."

"How?"

"A car wreck. Jake and Max were actually at our house when it happened. It was tough."

"Yeah, I hate that for them."

"Me too. But, well, you know, they've made peace with it. It's just taken time."

She forced herself to smile. "I'm glad. And glad y'all are close."

He smiled at her and ate a french fry. "So, let's talk about this house of yours."

"Yes, let's do." She pulled her thoughts back to her treehouse and smiled. Just thinking about her unique living quarters filled her with good vibes. "I know it's going to be fantastic."

And it was. Coming here was going to be fantastic…it was. She needed this.

She did. She just had to stay focused on why she had come.

CHAPTER FOUR

It was nearly seven when they climbed back on the Harley and headed back up the hill. Lilly was a bit of a mystery to Trent. She had chatted nonstop about her treehouse and what she wanted, declaring that she wanted him to use his creative ideas in the space. But then, right before they'd packed up and left the restaurant, a couple on the beach had seemed to snag her attention and she became quiet. Almost distracted.

The moment they pulled up to her trailer, she hopped off the motorcycle and handed him the helmet. "I'm excited about the treehouse. I can't wait. You just let me know whatever I need to do and I'm ready. But, I need to go inside and work. I...something I've been working on all afternoon just hit me back there at the Shrimp Shack and I really need to get it down on my computer."

"Sure. We have a rough design and I'll head back and work it out then show it to you tomorrow."

"Great." She was already backing toward the blue egg.

"You're going to be okay up here? Do I need to help set anything up for you?"

"Thanks, but I've got this. I've been setting up camp for years. Besides, I'll be moved into the cabin tomorrow. I'm excited about expanding my workspace in there."

He laughed as she bumped into the trailer and shot him a grin.

"I'm sorry, I get distracted when I start thinking about something good in my book."

"Looks that way. All right, talk to you tomorrow."

She gave a little wave, yanked open the creaky metal door and ducked into the interior of the blue egg.

That was different. He could only imagine how eager she had to be to get out of that thing. And she'd been living in it for years. That was something.

She was not a girl who required much.

Nope, no doubt about it: Lilly McCall was unique.

He drove home and parked the Knucklehead inside his garage and then closed the door and entered his house. He hooked his key on the keyring holder beside the back door, preoccupied as he headed into the kitchen and grabbed a bottle of water from the refrigerator. Opening it, he glanced around his fairly spacious home and thought of Lilly and her blue egg. *She needed space.* He moved down the hall to his small office—that had to be bigger than the entire space she was cramped up in right now.

Thinking about her made him smile as he turned on his computer. One thing was an absolute—this project wouldn't be boring.

Ever since he'd been released from the Navy SEALs, he'd been working on remodel jobs. He liked working with his hands but he loved taking a tree and creating a unique living space around the limbs.

His sisters had asked him to take on the remodel job of the Windswept Bay Resort when they'd decided to take it on after their parents had retired. Thankfully his sisters had understood when he'd turned them down and not pressured him to take on the job. It would've been a long, drawn-out project to be on for over a year, and it could possibly go for a little longer. It was a good-sized job and they had a really good man take over the job.

He just didn't want big, extensive projects. He wanted smaller jobs and treehouses were his love. And it had happened by accident when a client he was doing a bathroom remodel for on his ranch had, on a whim, decided he wanted a guest house built in a tree. He'd asked Trent to build it and that had started his passion for treehouses.

He opened up his drafting program and started to work.

He had thought about expanding the business and actually advertising what was till now a hobby. He just wasn't sure whether demand would be great enough, so for now a hobby worked.

The treehouses he'd built so far had ranged in prices from no-nonsense, bare bones homes to a more extravagant commercial guest quarters used as a bed-and-breakfast. Prices ranged from twenty-five grand to his largest, which had been about three hundred grand. That job took him six months but Lilly needed something soon, so he hoped mid-list was okay with her. It would have to be sufficient on their limited deadline and he felt confident, given her personality, that she would be fine with that.

He thought about her. She wanted nice and she told him that she wanted whatever he thought within the tree was unique and creative and would give her a view of the ocean. She wouldn't want extravagant but unique and he was determined to give that to her. He tried to do that for all his clients.

Ideas started to flow as he began work. It would be unique, like Lilly.

Quirky. Creative. Distracted. Distracting.

Beautiful. Curvy, womanly, sweet…Lilly.

Lilly beat the keys of her keyboard in a loud rap, rap, rapping noise. The words were flowing and she'd written most of the night. She loved it when the words came like this. At this rate, she'd finish this story in record time. Her shoulders ached and her head throbbed a little bit. A knock on her door rattled her, pulling her from the zone. Not that she wasn't able to jump right back into the story. She'd never have gotten anywhere with her writing if she hadn't been able to jump in and out of the word count zone. But still, she had been on a roll and she'd hoped hiding out up here in the hill side would give her peace to do her work.

She frowned when the knock came again.

"Lilly, are you in there?"

Trent. She glanced at her watch and gasped. It was eleven. The last time she'd looked, it was six a.m. It hit her then that she had to take a bathroom break. "Be right there!" She jumped up and instantly slammed her head against the cabinet above the tiny fold-down table that acted as her desk. Rubbing her head, she pulled open the door to the tiny bathroom that was not much bigger than the bathroom on a commercial airplane. She squeezed inside. This was her least favorite part of her tiny home. And she had to admit that now that she had a bigger place on the agenda, she was more than ready to retire her little home in exchange for one with a regular-sized bathroom. Moments later, teeth brushed and a brush raked through her curls, she admitted that until she got a shower and doused the masses with water there was nothing that could help the wild-looking woman who stared back at her. So, ignoring how bad she looked, she grabbed a bottle of water from the small, ancient refrigerator and opened the door. Trent stood with his back to the door as he stared across the clearing toward the tree that peaked above the others in the distance. *Her tree.*

When he turned to face her, she was reminded immediately what a handsome man he was. Her heartbeat kicked up its pace, letting her know that the attraction of yesterday was still strong today. She promptly ignored it. This was about a treehouse and that was that.

"Sorry, I was working and had to tend to a few things. Good morning." She hoped she didn't scare him off but the way his eyes widened momentarily told her he was startled by her appearance.

"Have you been writing all night?"

She took a long drink from the bottle and nodded. "I'm on a roll. The story is going great and I try to work as long as the words flow when that happens. It's one of the reasons I finally let go of my park service work—so that I could go with the flow when it happened. I loved my work with the national parks service and when I no longer needed the income, I gladly just volunteered. But I really enjoyed my last year of just immersing myself in my writing."

"I can't see that being good for you on a long-term basis."

She didn't point out to him that it wasn't his business to wonder such a thing. "I get my rest when I want to." She looked around at the forest around her and then at the small cabin. "I'm moving in there today, though. I've about had all the cramped up that I can take.”

He eyed her tiny trailer with a skeptical expression. “I can’t imagine living inside that tiny place for more than a short weekend.”

“I’ve done it. But you have to remember that I take all that outdoor stuff in my truck out and make an outdoor living space. And when I was working at parks, there are lodges and places I can hang out so I mainly use it as sleeping quarters. And sometimes sleeping quarters come with the job, if I opt to take it. Like at Yosemite. I stayed in one of their small places with a roommate they assigned me.”

“You must have loved it.”

She thought about it, thought about how it reminded her of her dad, made her feel close to him because their time as a family spent in the summers working at Bahia Honda State Park in the Keys had been some of her fondest memories. It had also given her the opportunity to be unattached.

“I did. It served its purpose.”

“I see. Well, I have your plans, if you want to look?”

"Oh, I can't wait. I'd invite you in here to show me but it would be like we were trapped inside a sardine can."

"It's okay. I'll use the tailgate of my truck." He strode to his truck and pulled down the tailgate. He laid papers out and Lilly moved close to look.

Her arm brushed his and a shiver of awareness raced through her, distracting her for a moment. But then she saw his drawing.

She gasped. "Oh, Trent, I love it." There were about five feet of stairs that led up to a walkway that wound through a few trees, and then more stairs that led up to a shorter walkway and then a few more stairs that led up to the landing of the treehouse. There was a note on the page that the water lines would run along the side of the landing up to the treehouse for the plumbing The exterior looked like glass and wood, with double doors onto the deck. The interior was open and there was a nice-sized bathroom and bedroom, and the kitchen and living space were connected. It all worked beautifully.

"You are a genius. It's beautiful. Now I see why

you took so many photos yesterday. It's beautiful but fun…I love the way it curves around the tree and the office on the second floor is perfect." Unable to stop herself this time she hugged him. "Thank you. I am so happy."

Only after she had her arms wrapped tightly around him did she realize what she was doing. She stepped away quickly and tried to ignore the buzz of butterflies she felt at touching him.

"I'm glad you like it. I have to finish up a job tomorrow and then I'll get started on it. How does that sound?"

"Absolutely fantastic. And now, I better dress and head over to find BJ and Olivia. I hope he's not out on his boat somewhere so that I can tell him I've moved into town."

"He'll be glad. He stays as busy as he wants to with his fishing tours, so you might not catch him until later in the day."

"Then, if that's the case, I'm opening up the cabin, unhooking from the trailer and going to find me some furniture if there isn't anything in there. They were supposed to have cleaned it but I never asked whether there was anything in it."

"So you haven't even looked inside?" he asked in disbelief.

"No, I meant to but then I got to writing and put it off." She started toward the cabin and reached behind the outdoor light beside the door and pulled a key off the backside. "Exactly where the Realtor told me it would be."

"So the writing thing—do you put everything off for the writing?"

She inserted the key into the lock and twisted as she answered him. "It's what I love." That was simple enough of an answer. There wasn't anything else in her life that held the same pull to her.

She pushed open the door and the lemon scent of furniture polish welcomed them. She breathed deeply. "I am absolutely going to get used to spreading out."

He chuckled and followed her inside. "It looks really clean. And you have furniture. At least something to start out with anyway."

She looked around at the small brown couch, the

brown chair, and the brown wood table. "Yes, really brown furniture." She laughed and caught his smiling eyes.

"Yeah, I wasn't going to point that out. But now that you mention it, I think they were very fond of brown."

"But other than that, compared to my trailer it is a palace," she said lightly. "I'm unloading my truck then heading to town to get some things I'll need. And hopefully see BJ. I really don't want him to find out from anyone else. Maybe I'll run by the resort and see if Olivia is at work."

"I'm sure she is. I've got a little time—let me help you unload your truck." He moved back through the door and she followed him as he strode toward her truck.

"It's mostly outdoor stuff," she said, though it was evident. "It won't take me but a few minutes to get it out."

He tugged down the tailgate. "Even less time if I help. Then you can head to town sooner."

"You're right. Thanks." She did need to hurry.

She wanted to find BJ and actually see him. It had been so long since they'd spent any time together. Within moments, they had the outdoor seating unloaded and arranged to the side of the cabin, along with the table and umbrella. He lifted her bike from the back and set it on the porch, out of the way of the door.

Once that was done, he looked around and gave a nod of approval. "So, see? That didn't take long. I'll head out now."

"Thanks. For everything."

"It'll be fun. I'm looking forward to it. But you are set up pretty good until we get the treehouse built. Oh, and just to warn you. I'm sure when Mom and Dad find out you're in town, they'll have a family gathering to welcome you to Windswept Bay."

Family gathering. "Oh, okay."

He studied her. "Everyone will be anxious to meet you and welcome you into the family."

"But I'm not family."

"You're BJ's sister, so that makes you part of the family. Mom is big on that. You'll see."

She hid her dismay as she waved and watched him

leave moments later. This was where holding back would be tricky. But, it wasn't as if they were her real family. She'd lost them. Nothing would ever be like that. Hurt that much.

So she really didn't have that much to worry about. *Right?*

Allowing herself to get close to BJ was the part that would really be hard on her heart.

That was the part she still wasn't completely sure about. But she had to try.

CHAPTER FIVE

Later, Lilly headed to town and went straight to the marina. She was in luck because as she stood there, she saw his boat come into the bay. Excitement filled her, seeing her brother's familiar form at the wheel. There were about five others on the boat, a group he'd taken out to deep-sea fish. She was sure they'd caught a load because BJ was very good at what he did. He loved it. He'd gotten that love from their dad. *Oh, how he'd loved being on the water.*

She placed her hands on her hips and watched as the boat drew closer. She wore cutoff jeans and a ball cap and had pulled her mass of curls into a thick ponytail. There was no way he would recognize her until he docked. And as he drew near, it was all she could do not to jump up and down and wave at him wildly. She hadn't realized until now just how much she had missed him.

When he had the boat maneuvered into its spot, he cut the engine and one of the men tied it to the pier. Everyone was chattering and laughing and happy as they poured off the boat and she watched as the familiar ritual began of them unloading the day's catch. BJ looked great. Seeing him smiling and happy jerked on her heartstrings and suddenly she was wondering why she'd stayed away from him for so long.

Unable to hold back any longer, she moved forward as soon as he'd shaken hands with the men and assured them that he would take care of cleaning their fish and having them shipped back to their homes.

"BJ," she called and he turned. His expression of surprise told her he'd recognized her voice even before he saw her.

"Lilly." He rushed to her, grabbing her and swinging her into his arms. "I have missed you, little sister."

His hug was warm and strong and sent waves of love crashing through her. "It's so good to see you, BJ." She held onto him. She laughed and tears dampened her eyes.

"I didn't know you were coming," he said.

"I know. I didn't want to tell you until I was here. You know me."

"Yes, I do. But you should have told me. I need to call Olivia. She'll be so excited. How are you?" He set her away from him but held onto her arms as he studied her. Concern etched his face.

"I'm good. I have a surprise for you."

He grinned. "Oh yeah, what? You're moving to Windswept Bay?" He laughed.

"I am. Or I have."

He went quiet. "You have? Already?"

She nodded. "I wanted to surprise you. So I bought a piece of property with a small cabin on it and

I drove into town yesterday."

"Yesterday—and you didn't call? You bought a place?"

She laughed. "Don't look so shocked. That's what I did. Just because I'm here now doesn't mean I'm letting go of control of my life," she warned him. "I have everything already figured out. I've moved here to be near you. To commit to rebuilding our relationship. I know my leaving after Dad and Mom died was hard on you but it's what I had to do. Now, I'm willing to be here and work through my issues. But on my terms."

He rubbed the back of his neck, strain evident in his features. "I know their deaths were hard on you, Lilly. I can't even imagine what you went through, trapped in that car, knowing they were dead and you not being able to do anything about it. I know. And I've forced myself to let you go. But I'm your big brother and you need to see how it is from my side. I lost them too. And I lost you that same night. I want you back. I want you in my life again, in my family's lives as I build one with Olivia."

They'd needed to say these things. She'd known it. Known she'd hurt him but known she'd had to do what she'd done. Part of her had died that night in that accident. A door had slammed shut and she had been physically incapable of feeling normal emotions. "I'm here to try," she said, softly. "But I'll still need my space. And I have a confession to make. I haven't been working for the park services for about a year."

"You haven't?"

She shook her head and told him about her writing. He was startled, as she'd expected, and then he smiled.

"It fits. I'm glad for you. I remember how you used to get lost in stories when we were growing up. And you could tell some really good stories."

She smiled at the memory. "I could spin some tall tales, that was the truth."

"So you're successful?"

"I actually am. And I love what I do. Everything about it. But I'll warn you that I get lost in my stories and I need time alone. So just because I'm here, don't think I'll be hanging out with you all the time or become your deckhand."

He laughed at that. Their dad had always teased her about being a really good deckhand when they'd spend their weeks at Bahia Honda State Park.

"Hey, I know you're very skilled at cleaning a boat deck after a day of fishing. Maybe you could help sometimes?"

It was her turn to laugh. "Nope. Sorry, boat cleaning days are behind me. But it's good memories." Her words trailed off and she thought of them as a family and the good times they'd had camping on that beautiful strip of heaven at the end of the Seven Mile Bridge in the Florida Keys.

"Yeah, good times. The best times were had there on the island." He pulled her back into his arms. "I am so glad you are here."

She felt the beat of his heart against her ear and let her arms go around her brother. She closed her eyes and hugged him as a lump formed in her throat. "Me too," she whispered, blinking heated eyes. She didn't cry, hadn't cried since that night in that car when she'd cried the tears of a thousand people. Still, her eyes burned and her throat hurt. She pushed out of his arms.

"So, where did you buy?"

"I bought a great spot. A really great spot. Do you know where Trent lives?"

He looked confused. "Trent? Olivia's brother?"

She nodded.

"Yeah, sure I do."

"I bought the lot at the top of that hill and hired him to build me a treehouse."

His eyes widened, just as everyone else's had. "Seriously?"

"Yes. I'm going to write in my treehouse from the top of my hill."

He laughed. "That's amazing. You are doing well?"

"I am. I love what I do, BJ. I can disappear into my books and create characters and take them on journeys to entertain my readers. I started writing on a whim one cold night on a snowy mountain and just wasn't able to stop. It has given me something I needed."

"Good. I'm glad. Now, I need to get this fish

cleaned up and packed and then we can go have dinner with Olivia. She's going to be as excited to see you as I am. I hate to make you wait but the catch needs to be tended to."

"I know. I actually have some errands to run. I can meet you later, if that works."

"Yeah, I'll call her, and then give you directions to the house."

A few minutes later, she parked her truck on the main drag of the cute beach town and went into one of the shops with colorful things. Bright colors drew her in and she found a pair of chairs and a couch that she knew would work in the cabin. She hadn't planned to get furniture—the brown would do—but once she saw the yellow and red toned plaid chairs, she hadn't been able to resist them. And then there was the red and white poppy covered couch…yes, it had to come too. She'd lived in that tiny space for so long, no room for anything and by her own choice. But now, she was expanding and bringing some color into her world, outside of the pages of her fiction. As she paid the man and set up the delivery for the next morning, she smiled as she headed back out onto the sidewalk. She saw a coffee shop and couldn't resist going inside to reward herself with a cup of coffee and a delicious scoop of coconut ice cream. She resisted the urge to buy a container of coffee for the house and headed back out onto the sidewalk, enjoying her treats.

Windswept Bay, with its pretty shops, beautiful backdrop of blue ocean, and laid-back tourist atmosphere was something she thought she could easily get used to. She needed to head to the grocery store and grab a few things but she found herself drawn to a seating area that overlooked the ocean. She sat down and savored her coffee and dessert. Her thoughts went to the book she was working on and she plotted out a few more scenes. When her phone rang, she jumped. It was BJ.

"How about us meeting Olivia for dinner at the resort? She's in the middle of a big project there."

"I'd like that. I've heard so much about the murals Grant Ellington painted at the resort. I can't wait to see them. I'll just meet you there."

"Sounds good. They're amazing. I'm on my way."

She walked to her truck feeling happy. There was just something about being here that felt right. She pulled into traffic and drove the three blocks to the beautiful resort that had been in BJ's wife's family since her grandparents had opened it. They had roots here that went deep and though she had no ties to the place except BJ, she was surprised by how much she was drawn to Windswept Bay.

CHAPTER SIX

Trent spent the afternoon at the remodel, going over his list of things to double-check before the owner came and gave his okay on the job. Already his mind was on the next job but he found it was more on Lilly than the actual project.

She had been totally unaware of him this morning when he'd knocked on her door. She'd been lost in her work. He understood that to an extent because when he'd started working on the treehouse design, he got lost in the creative part of that. He was glad she'd liked what he'd come up with so much.

He still could not fathom living in that matchbox-size trailer for years. He was climbing into his truck to leave when his twin brother Levi called.

"Hey, police chief," he teased when he took the call. "You ready for your hot date with that beautiful wife of yours?"

He had agreed to hang out with his new six-year-old nephew, Kevin, while Levi and Jessica went to a teacher appreciation dinner.

"Kevin is excited about you coming over. He wants to know if you will take him and the dogs to the beach."

"Sure. I'm leaving the Halberts' place and will swing by the house and change and be there within the hour. Tell him to get his kite ready."

"Already waiting by the front door for you." Levi laughed. "The kid thinks of everything."

"He's a cool kid."

"We think so. I'll let him know you're coming and going with his plan. Talk to you soon."

Trent clicked the call off and tossed the phone in the cup holder. Kevin had become part of the family when Levi and Jessica had married. The little boy was something, and an undeniable force when it came to getting under a person's skin. Everyone in the family was crazy about him and his mom, Jessica, since they had come into Levi's life. Trent was happy for his twin and despite guarding his heart, he'd let the kid wiggle past his barriers. He knew it was good for him. Knew that he couldn't hide his heart out forever. Where Kevin was concerned, the kid gave you no choice but to open up to him.

Kevin would be excited about the treehouse. He and Levi had built Kevin a small one in the tree behind their house and when he arrived less than an hour later, that was where he found him—looking down out of the window, waving a make-believe sword.

"He's been waiting up there for you," Jessica told him as she and Levi led him out onto the deck. "Get ready to squeeze your six-foot-tall body up there because he has drinks and a snack up there waiting on you."

Levi laughed. "Have fun. We should be home before ten."

"He'll need to be in bed by say, nine," Jessica added, giving Trent a hug. "That gives him a little bit of a late curfew for the two of you. He'll like that. Thanks so much."

"Anytime. He's a great kid."

She laughed. "Yes, he is. But he's got a mind of his own."

"Maybe he'll decide to set you up with someone." Levi winked. "It worked for me and this pretty lady." He pulled Jessica close and gave her a kiss.

Trent watched them and felt a tug at his heart. He was happy they'd found each other.

"You coming up here, Uncle Trent?" Kevin's impatient voice called and they all laughed.

"Your adoring fan calls," Jessica said. "Bye, honey. Have fun and be good for your uncle Trent."

The boy had his head stuck out the window opening. "I'll be good. We're going to eat our snack and then we're going to get going to take the dogs for a run on the beach. Right, Uncle Trent?"

"Right. See you two later. I've got business to tend to." Trent headed across the yard to where the two large dogs sat, looking wistfully up at the entrance to the treehouse. "Hey, boys. No pups allowed but give us a few and we'll head out." He scratched Rosco, Kevin's huge dog, behind the ears and then gave Levi's huge puppy a good rub too.

"Come on up," Kevin called, looking down at him with bright eyes.

Trent laughed, gave the dogs one more rub and then climbed the ladder. Both dogs whined as he left them behind.

"Don't worry, boys," Kevin told them. "Y'all get to go with us in a minute."

Trent stuck his head through the opening and looked around. "Hey, you've got a good setup in here." There was a fold-up chair in one corner and a small side table that came from Jessica's patio. It was big enough for two paper plates.

Kevin dropped into his small blue chair and grinned at him. The little boy was a small six-year-old who would turn seven in a couple of months.

"I made you a peanut butter sandwich," he said proudly. "I figured if we went ahead and ate dinner here, then we could go by and grab some ice cream when we got to the beach."

"You've got it all figured out. Ice cream sounds like a winner." Trent moved from the ladder to sit cross-legged on the wooden floor. He and Levi hadn't made the treehouse tall enough for them to stand up in, opting to keep the place more Kevin's size. He picked up the half a sandwich and took a bite while Kevin did the same.

"I was thinking we could build a baby bed in that corner. What do you think? I asked Mama if Aunt Jillian and Uncle Ryan's baby would be able to come up here in the treehouse after it's born but she said no, because it would be too little and had to have a baby bed. So I figure if we build it a baby bed then he can come up here. What do you think?"

"Oh, well, I'm thinking that a baby wouldn't really be needing to be up here for a few years. This is more for big fellas like you. It'll be best for the baby to stay near the ground."

"But he would like it up here."

"I'm not thinking he would. And besides that,

your aunt Jillian and your mother would probably freak out a little bit if somehow he was able to get up here."

"And that wouldn't be good. Okay, no babies allowed."

"There you go. In a few years, he can come up. So, you ready to head out?"

"I am. Got everything ready."

Trent smiled as they climbed out of the treehouse and headed into the house to grab the gear. They locked up, loaded the dogs into his truck and, with Kevin buckled into the backseat, headed to the beach. He glanced into the rearview mirror and smiled at the bright-eyed kid. Kevin chattered nonstop all the way to the resort.

Trent wanted kids of his own. The thought warmed inside him as he listened to his nephew's happy chatter. Something inside Trent was coming back to life and he tried hard not to fight it. It was time. He knew it. Knew that life couldn't stand still forever.

He pulled into the resort parking lot and drove to the far end near the back entrance to the beach area.

Within moments, he had the crew unloaded, and they headed to the beach. Bypassing the pool area, they skirted the outer edge of the resort and made their way to the large beach. He dropped the towels on a cabana chair and took the Frisbee out for the dogs and laid the kite for Kevin on the chair with the towels.

"We better give the dogs some exercise first." He laughed when they started prancing and jumping in an attempt to get the Frisbee from him.

"Yep, you better throw it or they're going to tackle you." Kevin laughed with excitement.

Trent threw it and the dogs took off after it. The pup was still clumsy; he was growing at such a fast rate that his motor skills couldn't keep up with his body. He tumbled in the sand as he attempted to make a dive for the disk. Rosco, however, big but full grown, dove into the air and snatched the yellow disk out of the air.

Kevin whooped and jumped and raced to his dogs, sliding in the sand and rolling with them with the joy that only a kid his age could muster. Trent chuckled and watched with his hands on his hips. Satisfaction warmed him as the trio jumped up and raced back to him. And so their evening went. Trent tossed the Frisbee more times than he could count. He raced down the beach with the kite and then tossed the laughing Kevin over his shoulder and jogged up the beach toward the resort to give him the ice cream from the resort cabana that he'd promised him.

Kevin laughed all the way while the dogs jumped to try to reach him. Once they reached the edge of the beach, Trent set Kevin on his feet and told the dogs to stay. They sat and watched with wishful expressions.

"I'll share with you," Kevin told them and gave them each a rub on the head.

The beachside restaurant was not too far from the outdoor cabana bar. When he heard his name, Trent glanced over to see BJ, Olivia, and Lilly at a table at the edge of the deck. BJ had risen and was waving at him.

"Hey," Trent called and looked down at Kevin. "Let's go say hi to everyone."

Kevin loved hanging around anyone in the Sinclair clan and once he saw BJ and Olivia, he took off toward them. Trent followed, his gaze automatically taking in Lilly. She was smiling and he was glad to see she'd finally met with her brother and Olivia.

They greeted everyone and Kevin got hugs from the group and an introduction to Lilly.

"You're pretty," he said without hesitation. "I like your hair. It's as curly as the curly fries I like to eat when I'm here. I like it."

"Well, thank you." She winked at him. "It gets pretty wild at times but I like it too."

Kevin reached out and touched a winding curl and grinned and then looked at Trent. "Hey, Uncle Trent, can I have some curly fries with my ice cream?"

BJ laughed and hitched a brow at Trent. "Y'all sit down. We're finishing up but not in any rush."

"Sure. Sounds good. I think I'll have some of those fries too. After all the exercise the kid put me through out there, the peanut butter sandwich he fed me in his treehouse has worn off."

That got a chuckle from everyone. There was only one extra chair at the table, so Trent grabbed one from the table behind him and when he turned around, Kevin had already sat down. Lilly was closest to him and scooted her chair over to make room for him at the table.

"So, y'all've heard the plan?"

"Yes, I told them. They're as excited as I am about my new treehouse," Lilly said.

"I am," Olivia said, laying a brief hand across the table to cup his arm as she smiled. "You are so good at that. And we are very excited Lilly is here."

"Thanks. I'm thinking it's going to be a cool project."

"You're getting a treehouse?" Shock widened Kevin's eyes. "One of Uncle Trent's big ones?"

"I am. It sounds like you have one too." Lilly gave her full attention to Kevin, and Trent found himself enjoying watching her. He'd thought about her off and on all day and was eager to start the job tomorrow.

"I do. You'll have to come over and see it. It's not real big but it'll do for now."

They all laughed at that. The waitress came over and they ordered the fries and a bowl of chocolate ice cream too. Trent figured this was a guys' night, so guys' food was okay.

He stood and leaned out over the rail to call the two dogs to come over next to the deck so he could keep an eye on them. Lilly reached over the railing and gave them each a pat.

"They are pretty."

Kevin proudly introduced them. "That's Rosco—he was my dad's dog. And when my dad went to heaven, Rosco became mine. And that's Jaco. He's my new dad's puppy that I got him to get. They get along real good. Just like me and Levi. My mom says we're all a match made from heaven."

Lilly's eyes widened just a touch and then she swallowed hard. "That's wonderful. So, your first dad is in heaven? I'm sorry. Mine is too. And my mom."

"Are you still sad?"

Trent saw the simple question from a little kid have the most profound effect on Lilly. He heard the slight intake of breath and saw a sadness sweep across her features like a rushing wind and then it was gone. If he hadn't been watching her so close, he might have missed it.

"I am sometimes."

Kevin studied her and then climbed out of his chair, walked around Trent to reach her and wrapped his arms around her. The action was so unexpected that Lilly's face registered shock as her gaze met Trent's. He saw them brighten with tears and his heart thundered and swelled.

"Hugs help. And it's okay to be sad. It just means you loved them." Kevin stepped back to look her in the eyes. "But it's good to be happy too because it makes them happy watching you."

Trent glanced at BJ and saw that he and Olivia had clasped hands on the table as he watched his sister.

"Thank you for that, Kevin," Lilly said, her voice thick. "I'll remember that."

His work done, Kevin walked back to his chair and sat down just as his fries and ice cream came. Trent's heart raced and he gave Lilly a small smile.

"Lilly told us she is a writer," Olivia said, refocusing the conversation. "And it turns out I'm one of her biggest fans. I love her Chloe Beck's books."

"It's my job for the next two months to give Lilly and her alter ego a fancy place in the trees to create." He really liked the idea more and more. He could see her up there, kicked back on her deck in the trees and looking over the treetops at the ocean. It really felt right for her. It fit her.

Kevin stopped a spoonful of ice cream midway to his mouth, his face scrunching as he thought. "I think I'll be a writer in my treehouse. But I'm gonna need to get better at writing first."

Olivia hugged him, a wide smile on her face. "Practicing your writing in your treehouse will help you get better. I think that's a great idea."

"Okay, but what is a pen name?"

"That's a name you use instead of your real name," Lilly explained.

"But why do you not want to use your real name?" Kevin asked.

BJ frowned. "Exactly what I'm wondering."

"There are lots of reasons. My reason is I didn't want any pressure from people around me knowing I was writing. Sometimes it's just better that way."

Later, after they'd all headed in their different directions and Levi and Jessica had come home and he was driving to his place, he had Lilly on his mind. She was a mixture of details, a puzzle that seemed to move around. He couldn't get over the way she'd looked when Kevin had hugged her. Or the way Olivia and BJ had looked. He was pretty sure he'd figured out that part of her puzzle went deep and stemmed from the loss of her parents. Losing them had affected her deeply and it might have been that part that drew him to her. He'd been affected irrevocably by losing Erica. He felt for Lilly and wondered whether she were here, trying to move forward. Because something about what had happened tonight told him that she hadn't yet, at least not prior to arriving here.

CHAPTER SEVEN

Lilly was thrilled when her new furniture arrived. She watched the two men carry out the brown couch and chairs and then replace them with the bright, colorful ones she'd chosen the day before. She clasped her hands together and rested her chin on her fist as she smiled at the way they looked.

"I have furniture. Real furniture." She sighed and then as the truck drove away, she did a little twirl and dropped down onto the couch. *It was amazing.* She kicked off her flip-flops and stretched out on the couch to stare up at the ceiling. *She had a couch.* And it was the most comfortable, beautiful thing she'd ever seen. She sighed with contentment. It was really hard to believe how easily she was taking to having her own space. It was clear that the timing had been right. Her heart was healing.

She blinked as she thought of that sweet child's simple and touching explanation of how he coped with losing his dad. He'd been so young. Looking at the ceiling, she blinked back tears once again. Yesterday when he'd hugged her, she had very nearly cried. It had shocked her at first, the feel of dampness there in her eyes. She'd felt the burn before but no tears had come.

Yesterday, as with now, she felt moisture. *Was that a sign her heart was coming back to life?*

There was another rumble of a vehicle and she sprang up from the couch and went to look out the window. *Trent was here.*

She had noticed him on the beach playing with Kevin as she and BJ and Olivia had been eating. It had been hard not to watch them romping and having fun. BJ had told him that Trent was turning out to be a great uncle. That he was normally quiet but that Kevin had been helping bring his quiet brother in law out some. It was obvious that he and the boy loved each other. And after she'd met Kevin, it was easy to see that it would be very hard not to love the child.

She wondered about Trent. *Why was he so quiet?*

As he drove past, getting the truck closer to the work site, she opted for her boots that were next to the door. Pulling them on, she hurried to go see what all he'd brought. Today was the day he started building her new home.

Her furniture was going to look even better up there in it when he finished.

He was loosening the tie-down straps from the sawhorses and boards and smiled as she walked up.

"Good morning," she called, clomping toward him.

"Good morning." He gave her a once-over with his eyes that twinkled and made her all too aware of the man. "Cute outfit."

She looked down at her normal writing attire: T-shirt, shorts, and boots. "Rule is never to tromp around the woods without boots."

"I totally agree. I brought you something," he said.

"Really, what?"

He let go of the strap and moved to his truck. Reaching through the open window, he pulled back and held out a paper coffee cup. "Wasn't sure if you'd want it but thought I'd bring it just in case. I was picking up a cup for myself and thought you might like it. The Gotta Have It Coffee Shop makes a great cup of coffee. Creamer and sugar are in the cup holder if you want some."

Lilly eyed the paper cup and then the man in awe. "You brought me coffee." She sighed and reached for the cup.

He grinned as their fingers brushed in the transfer of the cup.

That same spark shivered in her stomach at his touch.

"Yeah, I took a chance—"

Lilly ignored it and focused on the coffee. "You were right. Oh, how I've missed you," she cooed and took a sip. "It is delicious. I could kiss you for this."

He smiled sexily. "If you must. It's been awhile since a pretty lady kissed me."

She laughed. "I was teasing and I doubt very seriously it's been awhile."

He cocked his head to the side, those twinkling eyes challenging. "It's been awhile."

Lilly nearly got lost in the look in his eyes. "S-so, how about that treehouse," she managed and took a swig of coffee.

"Sorry, I couldn't resist teasing you. I'm setting up my work area. Is this okay with you? Out of your way enough? I'll come here to do my cutting. I'll be setting posts first."

She tried to get her thoughts off Trent. He *had* been teasing. "Anywhere is good with me. I'll be in there writing. Which I need to get back to. If you need anything, just knock."

"I won't need anything. You do what you need to. I'm fine."

She backed up with her coffee held tightly between both hands. "Great. Okay, got to go get my gal out of a burning house."

"Really?"

"Yep, left her about to jump out of a window over an hour ago. I got interrupted when my furniture arrived. You'll have to see it. It is so pretty. But anyway, I'll let you work and I'll go put a fire under my hero so he gets to my heroine in time." She swung around and tromped toward the cabin. *What was wrong with her?* The problem—now she wasn't thinking about her story hero at all. She was thinking about Trent and how good he looked standing there in that soft morning light. *Whew.*

"Hey," he called lightly.

She turned.

"Kevin enjoyed meeting you last night."

A warm fuzzy feeling went through her. "I liked meeting him. He's sweet. And you two were sweet out there on the sand playing."

"He's a fun kid. Been through a lot but doing good now."

"Yeah, I gathered that."

He stepped away from the truck and his expression was more serious. "I got the feeling, well, that he got to you a little bit. Were you okay?"

She swallowed hard. *He'd noticed.* She'd thought he had but wasn't sure. There was that moment when Kevin had hugged her and all her defenses had just dropped away and her gaze had met Trent's. He had noticed, saw her pain exposed. "I-I'm fine. But thanks for asking. Okay, see you later." She spun and didn't stop until she was inside.

The last thing she wanted was for Trent, or anyone, to see past her defenses. She'd work hard to keep them up. Kevin had just taken her by complete surprise. A kid—a little pint-sized boy—was the last person she'd expected to crack the shell around her heart.

But she'd be ready next time. Today, she had to focus, wipe out distractions, and get her writing done…

Trent worked all day, digging holes and setting the poles that would help support the walkway up to the treehouse. The lumberyard brought the lumber and stacked it for him and he signed the paperwork and watched them leave. It was nearly five when he called it a day, glancing at the cabin that had been closed up and quiet all afternoon. He thought about knocking on the door and letting Lilly know he was done for the day. But there really wasn't any reason to do that…other than to see her.

And that was *not* what he was here for.

Climbing into his truck, he backed around and then headed home. Only problem was he had Lilly on his mind.

When he arrived home, he took a shower and then took a ride on his motorcycle. He hoped the ride would clear his head but it didn't. At sunset, he pulled over on a shoulder overlooking the ocean and got off the Knucklehead. And he just stood there, looking out over the ocean as the waves rolled in below him. He breathed in the salt air and rubbed his brow as he thought about Erica. He'd loved her. And that day, when her team had gone out on patrol on a routine surveillance mission, they hadn't expected the sniper. Erica hadn't hesitated as she dove in front of the other members of her team. She took a chest full of bullets, giving them time to fire and take out the sniper.

Erica was dead before she hit the ground.

Even thinking about it all this time later, he nearly threw up. He'd loved her and she'd laid her life down for her team and if he'd been there she would have done it for him too. Or he would have done it for her. But he hadn't been there and it killed him. He closed his eyes, planted his hands on his hips and hung his head. Nothing he could do could turn back the clock and bring her back. Nothing he did could stop wishing it had been him and not her.

He couldn't talk about it. Didn't want to think about it. But she deserved to be thought about and remembered every day. And loved.

He needed to move forward with his life. Needed to find a way to let go but the guilt he felt for not being able to protect her wouldn't let him go.

And it felt wrong to want to let go.

Felt wrong to have Lilly on his mind like he had all day.

Restless, he watched the sun turn the sky an

amazing artwork of blue molded with splashes of orange and fading into a gentle pink….seeming to fight to hang onto the last threads of day, it finally dipped past the water. He stood there until the last of the light had ebbed from the sky and then he walked back to his bike and drove into the night. Nothing had been solved. *What was there to solve?* He couldn't let go.

Couldn't let her slide gently into the night like the sun had faded…she hadn't only died that day—she'd died for him. It wasn't something he could let fade away. It wasn't something he could seek to replace.

Not even if he'd been feeling the need to move on.

It wasn't right.

Despite knowing her almost irresistible neighbor and treehouse contractor extraordinaire had been working outside her cabin all day, Lilly was on a roll. And thank goodness for it. She'd promised to stay out of his hair, to let him get on with his work and by golly, she was going to do it. The fact that her book had taken on a life of its own was a very good thing. As she'd sat there, fighting the urge to go see whether he'd brought her a cup of coffee—strictly an excuse to go check him out that morning—her story-telling mind had taken a turn in the story that she hadn't expected and she'd dove for the computer. She loved it when her characters suddenly came to life in her thoughts and stole the story, taking her on their story journey—not the one she'd planned…not that she ever plotted extensively. But when her characters came alive enough in her head to take over the story, it was a treat for her because she was now on the same journey of discovery that her readers would be when reading it.

When these moments happened, that was when she disappeared. She drank hot tea and wished for coffee—pots of coffee—but it wasn't in the house, so she settled for the green tea and honey and pretended she loved it…*ack, ack, ack!* She ate peanut butter on a piece of wheat bread and truly loved that. She couldn't work on her writing sprints without her main food staple. The beauty of her bread and peanut butter: it worked for breakfast, lunch, and dinner…if she got hungry. But for the most part, she bent over her computer and she wrote, blasting the words out onto her keyboard with the force of a drummer pounding out a rock song with gusto.

And when—if—she got weary, she laid down for thirty minutes and then started again. Her mind only rested because it had reached its limit and then, until the words fighting to get out were out of her mind, fought the notion of sleep.

She lost sense of time. She got a call from BJ at some point and texted him that she was writing and would talk to him in a couple of days and then she blocked everything out. Even Trent.

Trent was finishing up work the following day. He'd managed to shake off his dark mood of the evening before but had been grateful for the labor-intense work of building the landing. He'd started working early. When he arrived, there was no sign of movement in the cabin and Lilly didn't come outside. He was tempted to knock on her door but didn't. *She was probably writing.* After all, he'd been afraid she wouldn't stay out of his hair, so he certainly couldn't bother her. Not unless he absolutely needed something and just wanting to see her was not an excuse.

With the measuring, cutting, and transporting the planks from his workstation to the treehouse site, he was in constant motion. And it had been good for him. He'd found himself glancing at the cabin over and over again and wondering how she was doing. By the time he'd loaded up and headed back to the house, it had been all he could do not to check on her. Her truck hadn't moved from where it had been the day before.

He told himself there was nothing wrong with a person not coming outside for twenty-four hours. And she was not his to worry about anyway.

He had a vivid picture of her in his mind, sitting at her computer with her fingers flying over the keyboard. He remembered how she said she got lost in her stories and he wondered whether that was what was happening right now.

Better to not disturb her.

Two hours later, he ate a simple dish of grilled pork off the pit and a baked potato while he tweaked the design of the treehouse. It was nearly eight-thirty when his phone rang. He glanced at the screen and saw it was BJ.

"Hey, what's up?" he asked the moment he had the phone to his ear.

"Trent, did you see Lilly yesterday or today?"

"No. I worked at her place but, well, I saw her yesterday morning but not before I left and not at all today. Why?"

"Look, I'm glad she's here but I'm in a bit of a spot here. She's as independent as it gets and I can't come barging in on her but I'm worried. I called her yesterday afternoon but she didn't answer the call and later sent me a message that she was working and was on a roll and that she'd call me in a couple of days. And nothing. I figured you might have talked to her."

Trent told himself not to be worried. "I'm sure she's fine. She told me when she gets on a roll or in the zone that she doesn't like to stop. Or be disturbed. That was one reason she wants to be secluded. I'm sure she's fine." He wasn't but BJ was right: they couldn't go knocking on her door every time she holed up. If they disturbed her right from the start, she might regret moving here.

"Look, is there something you can use as an excuse to go check on her? I mean, I thought she'd at least be around to watch you build her treehouse."

He had too. "An excuse?"

"Yeah, like a problem with the plans or something. Yeah, I could be overreacting. She's lived away from me for years and I should know to keep my distance but now that she's here…"

"I get it. We feel the same about Shar, Cali, Jillian, and Olivia. Believe me, when Olivia was living in Hollywood and didn't come home for a while, we were all ready to check on her. Brothers will be brothers. I'll figure something out. I'll call you if something is wrong. Okay?"

"Thanks, I owe you."

He was already headed out the door, keys to the truck in hand. In seconds he was backing out of the garage and heading up the winding road. He had no idea what he'd say to her but he figured it would come to him. He had the plans rolled up on the seat just in case.

Light glowed behind the window blinds but he couldn't see inside as he parked the truck. He strode to the door and knocked. When she didn't answer, he knocked again, remembering the first morning when she'd been writing in the trailer. It had taken her a few minutes. Still, worry set in when she hadn't answered on the third knock. He ran his fingers behind the light fixture, looking for the key, when the door cracked open.

"Trent. What are you doing?"

He glared at her, tried to hold back his worry and irritation but was sure it showed. "I was checking on you." The truth might hurt but he decided that was the right thing to do. "Can I come in?"

She backed into the room and held the door open. As soon as he was inside, she closed it behind him. He stared into her weary eyes and felt everything inside him knot up.

She looked tired; her eyes were red around the edges and weary-looking. "You look really tired. I haven't seen you for two days and it bothered me, wondering if you were all right. So here I am."

"I'm fine. I've just been working. I'm on a roll and this book is coming fast so I didn't want to stop."

"So you really do hole up and not come out?"

She nodded. "I told you that's how I like to do it when I'm in the zone."

He frowned. "But you're exhausted."

She might love what she did—there was no denying that, no way she could spend the time she spent on it without a passion for it. And the time obviously got away from her while she was in the zone, as she called it. No way could she do it that way and not love it. It was an odd combination, though looking at her and seeing the weariness but the enthusiasm in her at the same time—something in him liked that passion and energy rolled together in one beautiful package. But he also saw the obsessiveness of it and that worried him.

He swallowed hard as he fought the urge to reach out and push a strand of that crazy hair of hers out of her face. The want to cup her cheek overwhelmed him and he was hit with the sudden urge to plant a kiss on her soft, pink lips— He stepped back, yanked his gaze off her lips and to the kitchen counters in the background over her shoulder.

There was a container of peanut butter, honey, and a loaf of bread beside a cup with the string of a tea bag hanging out of it.

"Please tell me you've been eating more than that."

"Hey, don't put down my writing sustenance. Those four things there keep me going. Of course, I suffer through the green tea and honey. What really fuels me is my coffee. But I gave it up. It was so hard and I still crave it like mad. But I'd gotten up to three pots a day."

"Three pots?" He stared at her in horror.

She grimaced. "Well, actually it was four but I weaned myself down to three and couldn't get any lower—morning, noon, and evening. Ya know. What can I say? Anyway, the only recourse was to go cold turkey and get it out of the house. Now I only have coffee if I go to town and buy a cup. I do it as a reward. You do not know how lovely it was for you to bring me that cup the other morning. That's why I said I could kiss you."

He got an idea. "I get it now. And you're doing good, I gather."

"Better. It's a struggle sometimes. But when I get in the zone, I can forget about it and drink green tea with honey to give me a little energy…doesn't do what the caffeine does but it helps. And part of the addiction is simply the comfort of picking up a warm cup."

She was rambling and he could not help smiling. He also thought he knew just how to get her out of the house for a little while. "I suggest that you deserve a cup of coffee right now. You said you've had two very productive, creative days working on your book. And, though I don't drink coffee, I do think that I deserve a milkshake for working so hard on your treehouse."

Her eyes had widened as he spoke. *Had he completely lost his mind?* He needed to stay away from her on a personal basis but he couldn't resist the moment. And she did need to get out. And the way her eyes lit up did him in.

"I think that I could quite possibly love you," she

said with delight and laughed and headed toward the door. "Your ride or mine?"

He hurried after her. "Mine, though it's the truck."

"Oh, that's perfect because riding on the back of a motorcycle holding a paper cup of hot coffee is a little more dangerous and adventurous than I really care to be. And if we were in my truck, then I would be driving and I'm really not interested at the moment. Though I do truly enjoy driving. I want to get me a little convertible now that I'm here and I can scoot along the coast to town in it."

Okay, the woman completely boggled his mind. She opened his truck door and climbed inside, still talking as she slammed the door between them. He laughed as he jogged around to his side and climbed in—and yes, sure enough, she was still talking.

She was hilarious and cute and a bit out of her mind at the moment.

And there was no way he was backing out of this coffee run.

CHAPTER EIGHT

They picked up one large black coffee and one large chocolate milkshake at a drive-thru near the edge of town. Lilly rode beside him, slumped down in the seat, one hand out the open window to catch the air with her palm as she sipped her coffee contently. She'd needed this. Though riding beside a handsome guy on a winding drive along the moonlit coast sipping fabulous coffee was about the last thing she'd imagined happening tonight. It wasn't anywhere on her radar but she was doing exactly that.

"This is heavenly," she said with a deep sigh and

glanced over at her handsome treehouse contractor.

He stopped sipping his milkshake and brought it across the seat to tap lightly against her paper cup of coffee. "I'll toast to that."

She smiled at him. "Seriously, thank you. I'm loving this. It's a beautiful night."

The last thing she needed was complications involving their proximity after the treehouse was built, so she reminded herself that that meant hands-off. *What was it about Trent Sinclair that made her keep having to remind herself of that?* "I guess you could tell I was a little wound up."

"Yeah, I could tell. And I agree, you needed to get out. That can't be healthy."

She laughed this time. "So are you starting a neighborly trend? After you get my treehouse built, every few days you can come offer to take me for a cup of coffee and you get your milkshake—I'll buy."

"That sounds like a deal."

She looked away, suddenly feeling far too drawn to him. The ocean sparkled in the moonlight. Whitecapped waves faded to foam as they slipped inland on the sand and then headed back into the ocean. She wasn't ready to go home. "Do you think you have time to pull over? I haven't had a chance to dip my toes in the water since I arrived. And I really love a moonlit beach."

"Sure. There's a nice spot up ahead."

Moments later, he pulled off the road. "How's this?"

"Perfect." They got out and headed down the path.

She sipped her coffee as she followed Trent toward the ocean. She walked straight to the water's edge, kicked off her flip-flops and stepped into the cool surf. It lapped at her feet as she walked along, enjoying the refreshing feel of the water and the sand.

Now that he had both hands, he'd brought his plastic spoon and was eating the thick milkshake like ice cream. He paused his eating to study her. "Do you like to swim in the ocean?"

"Oh no. I don't go *into* the water, but I sure do like to have my toes in it."

"Oh, I see. Nothing wrong with that."

"Sure not. Is this section here usually vacant?"

"Sometimes. It depends on if it's the busy season. You know, during the day it can be busier but not many people come down here now. My brother, Levi—he's the chief of police—I wasn't sure if you remembered that—but him and his guys patrol down here a lot. He takes keeping Windswept Bay safe seriously. Partly because of him, Windswept Bay has remained a great place to live and vacation."

"I remembered. BJ said he was a great guy. He's the first one of y'all he met after Gage was shot. He really likes your entire family."

"We like him too. We're glad to expand our family to include him. And you."

"Oh, thank you." She looked away from him and took a long drink of her coffee and thought about being part of a family. The familiar panic welled inside her; she closed her eyes and willed it to go away. Willed it to ease out like the tide ebbing back out to sea.

"Are you okay?"

She opened her eyes and found he'd moved to stand beside her and was studying her.

"I'm fine."

"You just looked really sad just now. Pained might be a better word."

Her heart pounded in her ears and she breathed deeply. "I'm fine." The words were a mere whisper but at least she got them out.

He found himself watching her expressions in the reflection of the moon instead of watching the waters as they lapped at their feet. He tried not to stare but his eyes couldn't seem to obey.

"You're tired," he said. It wasn't his business but it was easy to see. And he thought something was suddenly bothering her too. *He should keep his mouth shut.* "Working that many hours just seems really hard on you."

She cocked her head to the side and looked at him. "When I've had enough, I quit. I'm not alone in how I work. A lot of authors do this. It's not uncommon."

"I understand that but that doesn't make it healthy."

"True. But I think maybe a writer's mind works a

little differently than some people's. When the story is working, or if a deadline is looming, it can get kind of manic in there." She tapped her temple and shot him a teasing smile. "And getting the book out is imperative. I can't sleep well. I don't want to sleep and trying to force myself is useless. So I go with it, getting the story down until either I'm absolutely too weary to go on or I'm done. That's how it is for me and many of my writer friends. It would drive me crazy if I couldn't get it put on paper or computer. I can't wait to do that in my treehouse. I just think it's going to be amazing."

"I hope so. And I understand you have this process, but you're single. What about when you have a family and kids?"

Her expression lost some of its animation and she looked back out at the ocean. "I don't know if I'll do that."

"Do that?"

"Have a family. Marry. I don't think that's for me."

He was startled by this revelation. "Is that because you don't want a husband and children to get in the way of your writing?" He couldn't help asking the question.

She bent to pick up a shell, glistening in the wet sand. "No, nothing like that. I just don't think family is for me."

Why did she say that? Could he ask?

She stood. "You asked me about family, now what about you? Is one on your horizon?"

Was family on his horizon? "I think so." He wanted it, if he could ever let go. Ever believe he had a right to one without Erica.

"Think so? You mean you're not sure?"

"Not really. I don't think you're sure either. I've been working through some…things. I'm—" He cleared his throat, now uncomfortable where this conversation had gone. "The last few years have been hard. I…" He didn't want to talk about this.

She was watching him thoughtfully. "It's hard sometimes to make decisions that have to do with the future. I know. I've been in limbo for years about it."

He knew how that felt. It dawned on him that she'd been through a bad loss. "How did you do after you lost your parents?" Her expression faltered and he wondered why he was asking.

She took a drink of her coffee and took a deep breath. "Not well. I have nightmares about it all the time. Even now. I haven't handled it well. At all."

Her words slammed into him. The impact was harsh. He hadn't expected her to say that. *And the look on her face...* "Why do you have nightmares?"

Her shoulders lifted as she took a deep breath. "You don't know?"

"Know what?"

"I was...in the car when my parents wrecked. It took hours before they were able to cut me out with the Jaws of Life."

"I am so sorry. I had no idea." His voice broke. *She knew. Knew the pain.* "How old were you?"

"Barely seventeen."

His heart hurt for her. She looked lost suddenly and he thought she was thinking about that moment.

"Maybe we shouldn't talk about this." She turned to him. "I'm ready to go home now." She walked past him, and after grabbing their shoes, headed toward the path to the truck.

He just stood there. "Wait." He jogged to catch up to her. Taking her arm, he gently stopped her. "Just wait a minute."

She stopped but didn't look at him.

He lifted his hand to push her hair out of her face so he could look into her eyes. Even in the low light of the moon, he recognized the deep pain. "You may not want to talk about it but do you *need* to talk about it?"

She inhaled slowly while holding his gaze. He fought the need to pull her close, to comfort her and bear some of what he felt certain she was holding in.

"I don't think I can."

"I understand better than you know. And if you decide you need to, I'm here."

The moment stretched and their gazes held and finally she nodded.

"Thank you. Now, I think it's time to call it a night."

"Your wish is my command." He gave her an easy smile as he waved his arm in a flourish, indicating for her to lead the way. He was glad as she shot him a smile before she started back toward the truck.

Trent was still thinking about the night an hour later as he sat on his deck and watched thin clouds play peek-a-boo with the moon. If there was ever a moment that had made it clear to him that a time would come when he was ready to move forward, to take that step toward a future he still didn't think he deserved but needed, it was those moments standing there, looking into the eyes of Lilly. *He wanted to move forward.*

And he wanted to do it with Lilly. Could he help her do the same?

It might not be easy for either of them and she might not want to move forward toward a future with him but all he knew was that didn't matter. What mattered was helping her.

But he couldn't help her until she was ready. Until she came to him and asked him or let him into her world.

If and when she did that, he would be ready.

CHAPTER NINE

Lilly had trouble focusing on her words the following day. She heard Trent outside working and wanted to go see his progress with every fiber of her being. But she had already opened up to him more than she was comfortable with and she was worried about that. Worried that she was building more of a relationship than she was comfortable with.

So she stayed inside. And thought about the way he'd so gently, and caringly, tried to help her. He had seen a part of her that she hid from everyone. *Why had she momentarily lost her footing in front of him? How had that happened?*

In part, she thought it might have been because she'd ventured into wanting to know his story. And in trying to understand the pain she'd glimpsed in him, she'd exposed her own.

Whatever it was, it had happened and she could not let it go.

As if on cue, the following evening BJ and Olivia arrived unexpectedly and knocked on her door.

She was startled when she opened the door to find them standing there. "Hi," she said.

"Hello to you, little sister. I thought we'd come over and see what kind of progress was being made on your treehouse. Want to show us?"

"I'm so excited about it." Olivia looked around. "It's beautiful up here."

Lilly stepped out onto the porch. "I'm glad you came. Come on. I actually haven't been to see it in a few days."

Olivia looked amazed. "You haven't? But why? It's right through there, isn't it?" She pointed toward the path that Trent had created through the trees.

"Yes, but I've been working. And I promised not to be in Trent's business all the time." She did not tell them that part of it was the fact that she was afraid spending time with Trent too much would lead to places she wasn't ready to go.

"Well, let's go see it," BJ said. "Trent told me he had the walk almost built and was working on the platform."

Olivia gave her a hug. "We also came to ask you if tomorrow would be a good time to have a gathering at Mom and Dad's with the whole clan, or at least everyone who can make it."

Lilly's stomach clenched. "Sure. That's great."

"Wonderful. I'll let Mom know. They are looking forward to meeting you."

"Likewise." She started toward the path, past the workstation Trent had originally set up.

They hadn't gone far before the stairs appeared up to the first landing that led toward the treehouse. She hesitated when she saw him hanging from the tree with a harness as he and another man worked on the floor of the treehouse. He held a nailgun in one hand; his shirt was stretched tight and his muscles flexed as he pressed the nailgun to the board and pulled the trigger. He worked with quick efficiency, taking the board that was handed to him and adding it to the floor. As she watched, he added three two-by-fours. They sat on the landing, waiting to be nailed on but it was quick work. It was easy to see that he had a routine on how he did this—but it wasn't his routine that she was interested in: it was watching him work.

She breathed in some fresh air and told herself to get a grip. This was about her treehouse. And the landings that he created were cool. She liked that to get to the tree she would be walking on elevated platforms. The very idea was neat to her. Trent waved when he caught sight of them. And she was very aware that butterflies lifted in her chest and fluttered their wings, as if running a butterfly race.

"Hey, Trent," BJ called. "Looking good—not you, but the treehouse." Her brother laughed and Trent gave him a thumbs-up.

Then, handing the nailgun off to his worker, he repelled down to the ground and unhooked himself from the harness. "Hey, you came to see it." He shook BJ's hand and gave Olivia a quick hug. Then he looked at her and cocked his head to one side. "So what do you think?"

"I like it," she said, feeling very self-conscious. This was the first time they'd seen each other since he dropped her off after their time on the beach. "I really like what you're doing. I love the walkway."

"Good. How's the writing going?"

"Good."

"That's good."

If they said good one more time, she thought that the grammar checker back at the cabin would haunt her. Striking repeat words was a big thing. But at the moment, it seemed to be the only thing she could say.

He smiled and those butterflies did some dips and dives and twirls that really bothered her.

Olivia saved the day when she lifted her finger and pointed at the platform for the treehouse. "That is going to really be a building in a little while?"

"Yes, it is. A nice building." Trent grinned at Olivia and then his smiling eyes met Lilly's. "I promise."

Lilly smiled and caught Olivia's curious gaze watching her, looking from her to Trent, and she knew exactly what BJ's wife was thinking. It wasn't hard to recognize two people struggling to force a conversation that was obviously uncomfortable to them. And it was probably very apparent, too, by the way that she was probably looking at Trent and the way that he was looking at her, that attraction—or the fight not to acknowledge the attraction—was the reason for the halted conversation. Her stunted conversation. She was socially inept at swimming in the waters of attraction. She wasn't even sure she was expressing herself in her own thoughts correctly. All she knew was that Olivia was trying to hide a smile because she recognized what was going on. She also knew that she could deny it all she wanted to, but she was very attracted to Trent. And then there was the fact that he had seemed to understand what she was going through. He seemed to have empathy for what she was feeling. That night, in the unspoken words between them, and standing here in the broad daylight, looking at him, she was drawn to him even more.

"Mom is having a dinner gathering tomorrow night—casual—but it's a welcoming party for Lilly. Can you make a trip?" Olivia asked.

Trent looked at her and nodded. "Of course I can. I figured it would be sometime this week—I wasn't sure what day."

"Yeah, I think it's going to be great. Don't you?"

Lilly nodded. *What could she say?*

"So when will the walls start going up?" she asked, trying to take focus off the awkwardness. She feared it was probably too late. But she could try.

He smiled and turned so that he faced the platform that his worker was continuing to work on. "It won't be long. Bill and I are moving along pretty well. We've been planning to have the flooring done over this week and then we'll start on the walls and the braces. It's a little different than building a house. And as you can see, since it is a little larger than your normal treehouse, we've added a few extra footings and those two posts will help give it a little extra support."

She had missed them hauling two very tall steel supports in and cementing them into the ground. *When had he done that?*

"From the looks of things, it looks like it's going to be massive," BJ said. "How big is this thing?"

She met her brother's questioning and startled eyes. "Not thousands of square feet. But by the time he wraps it around that tree and then adds to the top of it for my office and the small deck on the outside of that so that I have a nice view and a place to walk out on, it might be a thousand square feet with decking."

That was the size of an apartment. A huge apartment. It was far more than anything she had so far, living in her little trailer. And twice the size of the little cabin she was in now. It was the perfect size.

"I think it's going to be wonderful." Olivia stared at it and smiled. Then she looked back at her. "You're going to have to invite me over. I'm going to have to come and maybe even sleep over one night. Who knows—I might have to get my brother to build me one."

Trent laughed. "I've been building these for a

while, you know. No one has shown particular interest in it."

Olivia put a hand on her hip and cocked her head to one side as she met her brother's laughing eyes. "Until now. You might be about to go into business full-time building treehouses just for your family."

"That's fine by me. I really enjoy it. And this one for Lilly is going to be special."

Lilly couldn't help but smile. He was being so thoughtful in what he did with her place. And she really was grateful to him for that. He was being very considerate, helpful, and there was just no denying it: he was a very nice guy.

A little bit later, they left Trent and went back to her cabin. She showed BJ and Olivia the cabin, with her new furniture in it, and they got a glimpse of her messy desk with all of her yellow sticky notes everywhere and her empty bottles of water and the evidence of her holed-up existence.

BJ stared at her, curiosity evident in his eyes. "So

are you doing okay? It looks like you settled in quite nicely. I'm not gonna say the fact that you came here and locked yourself away like this doesn't bother me a little bit but I see what you're doing. And I'm just glad to have you around. But I'll be looking forward to seeing you at Violet and Sam's tomorrow night. So, again, are you doing okay?"

"I am. I'm doing fine. I actually live just fine. And a couple of nights ago, Trent came by and yanked me out of here because he had noticed that I was staying locked in here a little bit longer than he was comfortable with. I have a feeling you already know that. But we went and got some coffee. He got me out of here for a while and I actually enjoyed it." She did not say anything about the walk on the beach or their conversation. But she could tell by the way his expression eased that her brother was glad to hear that she had been out of the house.

"I'm glad you went out. I did ask Trent to look in on you. But I didn't know he was going to get you out of the house for a while and so I'm glad he did that. I think we both know that setting ourselves apart like we've done isn't the healthiest thing to do." He reached out and pulled Olivia close to his side and kissed her temple. Then he looked back at Lilly. "Olivia helped me understand that. I'm hoping that you'll be able to see that too. And get your work done. I like that you have this. Olivia looked you up on the Internet and it was really impressive—really, really impressive—about what you've done. I'm amazed. And very happy for you."

His praise sent a thrill of satisfaction through her. "Thank you. I love what I do. I loved working like a nomad for the park service like I did but it really wasn't anything that was completely satisfying to me. Writing satisfies me; it sends a thrill through me every time I release a book. And I get emails from readers who empathize with what happens to my characters or my stories. That means a lot to me when they tell me that my stories help them or inspire people. Sometimes they help people deal with issues that they're struggling with. Sometimes they just make someone laugh or smile or feel better about their day. I like that. It satisfies me in ways I never really knew that I needed to be satisfied."

BJ pulled her to him in a hug. It was brief but it was a good, warm feeling. He let her go pretty quickly, as if sensing that she still wasn't comfortable with that connection. "Mom and Dad would be happy for you too."

She smiled and thought about them. "I know. I feel them. Here." She thumped her heart, her throat clogged.

BJ nodded and then looked at Olivia. "I guess we better go."

"If you need us, call. And don't forget my brother is just down the road and right there building that treehouse. Don't be afraid to call him anytime you need anything. To be honest, your being here appears to be good for him too. He's our quiet brother. He's been that way ever since he came back from his military service."

"Thanks. He's helped if I needed anything."

A few minutes later, she watched them drive away. She waved and then as they drove out of sight, she stood there with her arms crossed and let the peace of her surroundings sink in. The sound of the nailgun made her smile. *Trent was getting her treehouse built.*

A sense of contentment washed through her. She liked the feeling.

Now she just had to make it through the dinner at Olivia and Trent's parents' home.

"Right now, you have to go write. Write and relax. It's going to be okay." *Right.* Thinking positive, she went back into the cabin and went to work.

She had barely sat down when there was a knock on her door. Startled, she walked to the door and pulled it open. Trent stood on the porch.

CHAPTER TEN

"Hey," Trent said, and instantly her thoughts were not on writing. Not on anything but the fact that she was glad he was there. Over his shoulder, she saw Bill driving out of the gate.

"Hey," she replied and he smiled.

"I'm about to leave but wanted to just touch base with you about dinner at my parents' place. Would you like to ride with me? I know you don't know the way and we're both coming back here."

"Sure," she answered instantly. "I mean, it makes sense."

"Exactly what I thought."

"Okay. And I really do like what you're doing."

"You know, you're welcome to come look any time you want. I never meant for you to stay away. It's your project."

"I know. I just have work."

"Right. How could I forget? Does every writer work twenty-four hours a day?"

"No. And I don't work that much. I do sleep."

"Not much, I'm betting."

She frowned at him. "Wow, I wasn't expecting to open my door and get a lecture. Maybe I'll drive myself tomorrow night." She started to close the door but he stopped her with a hand to the door.

"Wait. I didn't mean that. I just worry about you and it's taken everything I have since the night on the beach not to come here every day and make sure you're okay. Today was the first time I've seen any movement here. I wanted to ask you out for coffee but figured asking too soon might get me turned down."

"I thought we decided you could come to my rescue anytime with the offer of a cup of coffee and some fresh breeze blowing through my hair."

"You're right. But then, that night got pretty

intense there at the end and I worried that if I came too soon you'd think I was pressing you about opening up."

She had lain awake that night, her thoughts on Trent and how gentle he'd been when she'd been thinking about her past. She'd effectively pushed it to the back of her thoughts with focused effort. But it hadn't been easy. "I, we, did get into some deep waters. I'm fine. So don't worry about it."

His brows knit together. "I'm not going to push. But...okay, never mind. I better go. I'll be working tomorrow and I'll head home about four-thirty and then come back and pick you up around five-thirty. I think dinner is around six. Always is."

"Okay. Thanks."

He gave her a thumbs-up and then strode from the steps and to his truck. As he drove away, she breathed a sigh of relief.

Trent arrived back at Lilly's at five-thirty the next evening as planned. He'd worked hard all day getting the floor finished and had harbored hopes that Lilly would come show her pretty face at least once during the day. But again, no. He had completely misjudged her from the first day that she'd come into his life. From thinking she was going to be too involved with the project to her being almost not involved at all, it was really surprising. But then, she was on her deadline. And it really wasn't any of his business. He reminded himself of that all day.

Bill had given up trying to have a conversation with him after several tries. And he'd told Trent his mood was pretty rank. Trent hadn't meant to be moody, but he was frustrated. He and Jacob worked well together most of the time because they were both fairly quiet, so it hadn't been a big deal.

Still, as Trent stepped onto Lilly's porch, he was ready to see Lilly. She swung the door open before he had time to knock. And she took his breath away. Her curly hair was pulled into a messy bun thing on top of her head and curls cascaded down everywhere. She wore a sundress that had a scooped neckline and was a rich yellow, shot with gold and orange. Her sandals were golden, with tiny sparkles on them. She looked cute and pretty and sexy at the same time. She took his breath away. He swallowed hard. "You look beautiful," he blurted the instant he saw her and felt a little tongue-tied.

She splayed a hand over her stomach as if to calm her nerves. "I'm hoping I look okay. I wasn't sure what to wear and so I dug this out and ironed it."

"Our family gatherings are real laid-back so anything would work. Believe me, you're more than fine."

"Thanks. I have to admit this is making me really nervous."

"Why? My family is great. And we love BJ. He's like a brother already. We've lucked out on all the guys our sisters have married. You'll be okay. Really."

She didn't look convinced. "I'm glad you offered to pick me up. I honestly thought about canceling."

She was serious. It dawned on him that she'd spent a lot of time avoiding contact with her brother after losing her parents in that car wreck. "How old were you when you went to work with the parks?"

"I was still seventeen. BJ didn't like it at first but there was nothing he could do to stop me."

"So you left not long after the wreck?"

"I did. I had to. I needed to get away. I went to Bahia Honda State Park in the Florida Keys with BJ not long after the funeral. That was our family's happy place but I just couldn't cope. I was having nightmares and constantly worrying about when something was going to happen to BJ too. In the end I just disconnected, it helped me function better. I had often hung out with the park workers when we had been there on vacation and I just needed to disappear. Working in parks worked for me."

He was beginning to understand better and better about what had gone on. He couldn't help himself—he stepped forward and gently turned her to him; he wrapped his arms around her and held her. She laid her head against his shoulder and he could feel her heartbeat thundering against his. *What had she gone through?* The trauma that she had felt was only now really sinking into him. That night on the beach, when she first told him, he thought he understood. But it went even deeper than he had anticipated. She was still suffering. And the anxiety was written all over her face. All over the stiffness of her body and in her words. And all he wanted to do was help her overcome it.

"I'm here if you just need to talk. It's gonna be okay. You went through something that no one should have to have gone through. Are you afraid of losing someone you love again?" He knew that had to be what it was. He understood it. He felt it. He felt it on that night on the beach when she first told him what she'd been through. They connected in the end; he wanted to make sure she completely understood.

"I want to tell you that I lost a fiancée on the battlefield. She died after diving infront of her other team members and taking bullets.. Losing her set me back, really set me back. It's taking me a long time to overcome it. This hilltop has helped me. This place. Taking one day at a time. But I can tell you I have a fear of losing someone I love the way that I loved Erica. I have a fear of ever giving my heart to someone and then something horrible happening. Of not being there to protect them…I wasn't there to protect Erica. So I've taken my time. I keep my stress levels low. And my family has just been there for me. I don't know that I could've made it through all this time without the knowledge that my family was there, giving me my space, giving me time. But the knowledge that they were there was comforting. Not terrifying. The terrifying part was, could I ever let myself fall in love again and risk that kind of loss? Even more the question was, did I deserve to ever find someone to love again when Erica was dead?

"I think your brother is giving you space—has given you space. And is waiting patiently. I hope you know—I'm pretty positive I know—that he would be there for you in an instant. But I'm really glad you came to Windswept Bay." His heart thundered. He didn't want to scare her off. He just wanted to help ease her back into living a life, a full life that was healthy. He was convinced that what she was doing to herself right now was not healthy for her; it was her way of hiding. But he stayed away from that subject. With time, maybe there would be a balance for her.

"You just need to breathe and take it one step at a time, one day at a time. Don't put pressure on yourself. I promise you there is no pressure from my family. And what I've learned and, it's clear to me every day, is that love is a wonderful thing. The threat of loss is terrifying and if it happens, it's, as you know, horrifyingly painful. But the beauty of it is that you are loved. Your parents wouldn't want you to continue suffering over their loss. I'm quite sure that they would want you to move forward. Healthy and with an open heart."

Her arms tied around him and she just held on. They stood there for a long moment; she still hadn't said anything.

"Thank you. I'm terrified. And I haven't told anyone that I haven't talked to anyone."

"Then I'm glad you're talking to me."

She lifted her face and he saw her eyes sparkled with the threat of tears. But he realized he hadn't seen her cry. "Thank you."

He couldn't help himself; he kissed her forehead. He wanted to kiss her lips but now was not the time.

"You're welcome. And seriously, thank you for talking to me. It means a lot to me. You mean a lot to me. In the short time that I've known you, I feel more connected to you than I've felt to anyone since the loss of Erica. I'm not saying that to scare you. I'm just being honest. I hope that you can be honest with me. I want to help you—however and whatever I can do, I want to help you. No strings attached—nothing. I just want to help you. I want to be your friend."

"Thank you again. I'm going to need a friend."

He smiled at her. "You got it, babe." He kissed her forehead again and gave her a tight hug. Wishing he didn't have to let her go. "So, are you ready to go do this?"

Lilly's knees melted and she tried not to wish Trent's arms could stay around her forever or that he'd kissed her lips instead of her forehead. But she did wish for all of that. Not only did his actions send her stomach into somersaults they gave her a sense of security. This was a step she needed to take. She knew it and she was grateful for his support. Looking into his reassuring gaze her world steadied and she inhaled a fortifying breath full of his masculine scent. "Ready as I'll ever be. One step at a time."

His lips curved upward. "There you go. Just ease into this."

And then he let her go, but he took her hand and they walked to his truck together.

Minutes later, they arrived at his parents' home on the other side of town. Several cars were already there and as they got out of the truck, her stomach felt queasy. But she reminded herself that she was just meeting BJ's family, that was all. *Family.* Her heart thundered as the night of the wreck flashed through her mind when she lost her family... She stood there on the driveway, frozen.

"Are you okay?" Trent's gentle voice brought her out of the horror that almost pulled her under. "Lilly?"

She nodded and met his worried gaze. "I'm fine." She took a deep breath and forced herself to take a step forward. "One step at a time," she barely whispered.

"One step at a time. You're doing good."

Her eyes dampened. "Thank you for being here."

He winked at her. "I'll be right beside you."

And he was.

Trent's parents were a handsome couple. His dad, Sam, was tall; Trent and his twin, Levi, resembled him. Violet had beautiful, long silver hair and a warm smile. She welcomed Lilly with a hug, which caught Lilly off guard and had her remembering the feel of her own mother's arms holding her tight. And they welcomed her as if she were their own.

"I hope you're hungry. I'm grilling up enough to feed an army," Sam said.

"I am hungry." She was starving but was sure her nervous stomach couldn't tolerate anything.

"Good, good. I've got to get out there and put this massive platter of barbeque on the pit but when you can find a free moment, come out and tell me about this treehouse project you've got Trent doing for you."

"Okay, I will." She watched him head for the double glass doors that led to the patio.

"Let me get the door for you, Dad." Trent opened the door and let his dad pass through.

"Thanks, son. Gage, can you grab the tray of condiments and we'll get this party rolling."

"Got them, sir," Gage, Shar's husband, called and caught up, carrying a tray with all kinds of ingredients on it. "Don't worry, everyone. I won't add anything to anything unless Sam tells me to. I'm a grilling beginner."

"That's great, honey. Learn a lot." Shar turned to Lilly. "He's never grilled much. Always stuck inside a skyscraper, making big deals. So he's playing catch-up on the outdoors stuff."

Lilly had only begun to realize how very different her brother and his new half-brother's life had been before they'd learned about each other only months ago.

Violet beamed. "And Sam is loving showing him all of his secrets."

Olivia chuckled. "Seriously. Dad is certainly the one to learn from. He's really amazing at grilling. He makes a special sauce I've finally convinced him to let me have produced so that we can market it in the Windswept Bay Resort gift shop and also use in the kitchen on a dish we're going to name after him. It's taken some convincing but it's the right thing to do. Wait till you taste it."

Lilly was now very interested in Mr. Sinclair's BBQ sauce. "I can't wait."

Jillian was arranging cake on a platter on the kitchen bar. It was easy to tell she was pregnant. "Olivia is really putting her marketing degree to use now that she's helping with the resort. She just recently moved back and meeting BJ helped keep her here." She paused in her cake arranging. "We are very grateful to your brother for winning her heart and giving her a reason not to return to Hollywood."

"I'm glad he found Olivia too," she agreed.

"You are no happier about it than I am," Olivia chimed in. "Especially since you and Ryan are going to be making me an aunt in about two months. Biggest event of the decade!"

"I was about to ask about the baby. So you're about seven months?" Lilly once wanted children so badly. As a girl, she spent hours of her day playing with her pretend babies. But now…like she'd become about everything, she had to overcome her past.

"Not quite. Another two weeks and I'll be there. This baby girl is just tiny, so I'm not all that big. But I have a feeling I'll balloon next month. But that's fine with me as long as she's healthy."

Lilly nodded and caught Trent watching her. He gave her an encouraging smile and she smiled back. The evening moved along and she got to meet everyone. She felt very welcomed and she tried to not let her stomach get to her. But the longer the evening went, the more she knew she might be in really big trouble. Because what she quickly saw was that the Sinclair family was a caring bunch who immediately treated her as one of their own. And she saw that it would be very hard not to care for them.

A longing awakened in her heart for what they had. What she'd lost...people who would care whether she got home okay after she left them. Or people who just wanted to listen to how her day had gone. And everyone wanted to know about her books. The girls had already looked her up on the Internet and ordered copies to put in the resort gift shop.

"People always need a good beach read," Cali said. "Would you mind autographing them when they arrive? If that's not asking too much."

"I'd love to. And thank you for thinking of putting them there."

"Oh certainly. It's a real treat," she said.

"I'm reading one," Shar said. "And really enjoying it."

Lilly got the feeling that Shar never said anything she didn't mean. So she felt honored by her comments.

"I'm glad." Lilly enjoyed meeting all the sisters and seeing their different personalities. Despite the fact that Olivia, Jillian, and Shar were triplets, Cali, the older sister by a couple of years, was blonde and looked more like the third triplet than Shar did. Shar was dark-haired and had a very vivacious personality, much different than the other three sisters. She thought Shar looked more like Violet but that the other three had their mother's personality.

Lilly thoroughly enjoyed meeting them all as a group.

Cali's husband Grant, the famous artist, came over

to meet her. She was intrigued with his art as he was with her books.

"I love your paintings. I saw the murals you painted at the resort."

"I hope you liked them. I'm always proud to draw attention to the sea life with my work."

That led to a conversation about the sea turtles and Shar's work with the Windswept Bay Sea Turtle Hospital. This intrigued Lilly.

"I love getting people involved with my passion for sea turtles." Shar's eyes came alive as she spoke. "Have you ever thought about writing about them?"

Lilly's mind was already rolling with thoughts about it. "I remember when my dad and my mom would take me and BJ on vacation to Bahia Honda State Park in the Florida Keys. I loved it there and we would spend several weeks there on vacation. It's just on the other side of the Seven Mile Bridge and Marathon Key has a sea turtle hospital. Dad took us there. I loved it. I've been thinking about setting a series around the Keys, and incorporating the sea turtles would be perfect. Several times they rescued turtles while we were there and several times they held sea turtle releases, letting them back into the ocean after they were healed. It was always a great feeling to see those huge, gentle creatures swim back to their natural habitat. Would you mind if I came to the hospital for a tour?"

Shar's expression lit up. "I would love that. Anything at all that brings attention to my sea turtles will be fantastic. Maybe you would like to go with me on a morning run along a beach. I go somewhere every morning to check out the beaches."

Jillian had been joining the conversations at times. Now she hugged Shar. "This is our Superwoman," she said, clearly proud. "She takes a run every morning on one of the different beaches, in search for nest of babies or injured turtles. No one cares for them like Shar. She's amazingly dedicated."

Lilly was completely drawn to what Shar was doing. "That will be awesome. I would love that very much. I'm finishing a book now and I'm very close to the end. I've been very on fire with my word count since moving here, so I'm ahead of schedule. If I push myself, I can be finished with it maybe in a couple of days. And then I would love to go with you to check out the beaches for research."

She could see Trent, not too far away. He was talking with Levi and BJ. He turned to look at her. His smile was wide, obviously having heard the conversation; he winked at her and nodded. She knew he liked what she had said very much. She smiled at him and her heart warmed.

Shar was just as excited too. But the night didn't stop there. When Max and his new wife, Kelsey, arrived, she invited Lilly to come out to the horse stables that she ran for Cam. "If you've never ridden a horse on the beach, you're going to love it."

Max nodded his agreement. "I can vouch for that. And Kelsey is a great teacher, and I'm not just saying that because I love her. She's fantastic. I love watching her work with the kids she teaches."

Lilly loved the idea. She had never ridden a horse much at all and especially not on a beach. It was obvious that Max was crazy about Kelsey.

"I'll do that, just as soon as I can." She caught

Trent watching her again and suddenly she got the feeling he might have asked his family to extend these invitations to her. But then again, they were all very genuine. He had thought of every way possible to help her feel comfortable. And it hit her that this outing had become different than what she had anticipated. It hit her that she was no longer nervous or anxious. She had crossed into actually enjoying herself. *How had that happened?*

Jessica and Kevin arrived late; they had been at a birthday party Kevin was attending. She gave the kid a hug.

"I want Uncle Trent and Uncle Jake to come play with me and my dogs. You want to come play with Rosco and Jaco and me?"

His huge dogs ran on the beach and she could see them through the glass windows overlooking the beach. "Sure. I'd love to."

And so she found herself outside on the beach with Trent and little Kevin and Jake, who had been running late, too, because a diving trip had extended longer than he'd planned. It was obvious as she watched all the guys romping on the beach with Kevin and the dogs that they all enjoyed little Kevin. And the kid enjoyed them. She had never heard so much laughter. The dogs barked and ran and Kevin threw her the Frisbee. She jumped into the air and grabbed it.

"Run," yelled Kevin, jumping up and down and waving his arms.

She did as he told her and plowed forward. The dogs loped beside her, barking, and then Trent overtook her and snagged her around the waist and picked her up off the ground. She was laughing hard when Jaco moved into Trent's path and they tumbled to the sand. She rolled one way and he rolled the other. And the large yellow dog bounded over to look down at her. Trent rolled back toward her, smiling like a kid having a grand day on the beach. He looked so alive with his dancing eyes.

"Are you okay?" He rose up on an elbow to look at her.

She sat up, her heart racing. "I'm great. I'm having so much fun."

Kevin dove onto Trent's back and the dogs piled

on top of him. She and Jake watched as Trent got Kevin on his back and tickled him.

"Uncle Trent." Kevin giggled, grinning at her. "I like Lilly. Do you?"

Trent looked at her and his expression turned serious. "Yeah, I like her a lot, Kevin." His gaze locked onto hers.

Butterflies churned in her stomach as she took a deep breath. Jake reached down, picked Kevin up in his arms and threw him over his shoulder. "Let's go, kiddo. It's dinnertime. We'll catch you two in a few minutes." He shot them a grin and then jogged away with the giggling kid dangling over his shoulder.

Trent smiled at her. "He's a great kid," he said, and then his tone softened. "So how are you doing?"

"I'm doing okay. Your family is great."

"Yes, they are. But I know this is hard on you. Are you making it okay?"

"I am. I never wanted you to think your family was what worried me in a bad way. It's exactly the opposite. I'm worried I could get attached to your family, BJ's new family. I'm not sure."

It was the truth and she didn't know any other way to put it.

Trent hurt for Lilly. She had no idea how stricken she looked.

She cleared her throat and her lip trembled and he ached for her. "I'm not sure I could ever open my heart to another family I'm terrified of losing again."

Trent couldn't help himself; he cupped her chin with his hand and gently ran his thumb across her soft cheek. "I know. I figured that out. I've had the same issues. We talked about this a little. I lost Erica and I've never thought I could deserve, or want to love someone again. But mostly I've never thought I could let myself love someone again and then lose them. I feel exactly the way you do. Loving someone is to lay our heart bare, to open it up not just to the promise of love but also to the threat of loss. Love and loss go hand-in-hand. We both know that."

She nodded, hearing his words and knowing he was hitting at the core of her trouble.

"Lilly, you lost your parents. You lived in the horror of that moment when you lost them. You couldn't get to them, you couldn't help them and you had to lay there and know that. It's hard to get over."

"Is that how it feels for you too?"

"It is in many ways. I would have gladly taken those bullets for Erica if I had been there. She took the hit on purpose. And I live every day knowing that I wasn't there for her and it kills me. But you know what I figured out because of you? Lilly, she did that because of the person she was. She was brave and strong and gave her all for her country and her fellow team members and she made that split second choice. But I wanted her to live and she would have wanted me to live because she loved me. But I haven't been able to, not fully. Since meeting you, for the first time I actually want to live fully again—no strings attached. I'm not telling you this to scare you or to make you uncomfortable. I'm just trying to get across to you that your situation has opened my eyes and I can tell you that Erica—I know her heart and she would want me to move forward and not waste the gift she sacrificed for

me and everyone else that day when she gave her life."
He paused taking it all in.

"She would have," Lilly said softly.

He willed her to see the truth. "Your parents would want the same for you. They would not have wanted it the other way, for you to have died and them to have lived. Not if it had to be one way or the other. How do I know that? Because you were their child. And to know you is to love you. And so I'm hoping that you'll relax and just let yourself live again. Loss is natural, tragedy is not, but you have to pick up after it. You have to move forward, for all those involved. That's how I feel about it…now. Now that I see clearly with my heart. Let's just go in and enjoy the meal, if not for yourself, then for BJ. And then I'll take you back home and you can relax and write—because writing is your comfort zone. And you can just ease into this new life. And if you can't embrace everything, just embrace what you can. But I hope you won't run away from everything."

He let his thumb softly trace across her cheek one last time and then he dropped his hand. He didn't want to pressure her or to scare her any more than the words he had spoken might have already. And he could tell by the look on her face that she was uncertain, but he thought maybe she was also thinking.

He wanted more, but there was no way he was going to pressure Lilly.

"Thank you," she said softly. "Please don't fall for me. I can't promise you anything. And the last thing I want to do is to hurt you. I'm drawn to you, Trent. There's no way I can deny that. But I am damaged. Broken in so many ways."

"One day at a time."

She swallowed hard and looked away for a brief moment before she met his gaze once more. "But I'll keep taking one day at a time. So let's do this."

He smiled. "That's the woman I know." He stood and held out his hand to her. She slipped hers into his and he tugged her to her feet. Every fiber of his being wanted to pull her to him, to kiss her sweet, soft lips and to hold her close. But he couldn't crowd her. Not with all she was dealing with.

For now, he would just be here for her.

CHAPTER ELEVEN

Lilly stared at her computer screen, rubbed her eyes and then typed "The End." She was done. Her eyes hurt and were scratchy, and she needed eye drops. She needed coffee but she needed sleep more.

Leaning back in her chair and stretching, she glanced at the clock and date on her phone and then shook her head. It had been five days since Trent's parents' party. She'd been upset when she'd arrived home but held it in.

It had been a very hard evening for her. Trent had been so understanding, so very gentle. And his thoughts had been so clear when he'd taken her hand and led her from the beach back inside to join the dinner. She'd forced herself to relax—no, not really: she *had* relaxed.

It was just hard to admit that she'd enjoyed herself.

The fact that she'd relaxed completely amazed her. The food was great and she really enjoyed spending time with everyone. Though she felt guilty for having had a good time.

She tried to push the guilt aside and told herself this was normal. She had to move on with her life.

But first she would get some sleep. She headed into her bedroom, crawled into bed and closed her eyes.

By the morning of the sixth day after the party, Trent was having to force himself to work. Since dropping her off after the party, he hadn't seen her and it was all he could do to keep from banging her door down. He was loading his truck and about to head up the hill when BJ called.

"Have you seen her yet?" BJ's voice was harsh, irritated. It sounded exactly how Trent felt. BJ had called nearly every morning and Trent had talked him into not going and bothering Lilly. This morning, he said the same thing he had said every morning.

"I haven't seen her, BJ. But she needs time. Your sister is dealing with a lot. More than you can imagine. She's one strong woman, though."

BJ was silent on the other end of the phone. "Olivia said Lilly watched every move the family made like a hungry person. I'm worried about her."

"Just be patient. Give her a little more time. She made some progress at the party. It can't happen overnight."

"I get that. I want Lilly as part of my life."

"Then don't you run her away. Don't run her off."

"Okay. But if she's in that house and she's hurt and she needs help—"

"She's a healthy person. And she's not going to hurt herself. She's trying to finish her book. And I'm convinced she needs to write. Have you read one of her books since learning her pen name?”

“No, I haven’t. Olivia read one and said it was good.”

“They are. They’re about love. But her stories are also about community. She has a community in her stories. And family in her stories. Do you hear what I’m telling you, BJ? She’s created what she’s missing in her books. She goes to her books for what she needs. Family, love, nurturing, healing. I think she came here, knowing it was time to move forward and she will. You just need to give her a few more days.”

“Okay. A couple more days and then I’m coming over there.”

“I hear you.” Trent hung the phone up after BJ said goodbye. He stood there on the drive for a moment, looking up the hillside. And then he got in his truck and went to the coffee shop.

By the time Lilly woke up, it was seven a.m. on the sixth day after the party. She stretched and then jumped in the shower and dressed for the day. She felt energized as she jogged down the path to see what kind of progress Trent had made while she was pounding the keys of her computer. She almost tripped over her feet in surprise when she saw the treehouse was completely built on the exterior. Even her upper floor had walls. The man and his team of one, Jacob, had been pounding boards almost faster than she'd been typing. It was amazing.

And it was beautiful. She jogged up the first flight of steps and then jogged down the walkway and up the next flight. Then jogged to the next flight and walked up the final flight so that she could step out onto her deck. Her heart thundered with excitement as she turned and looked down at the ground and the undisturbed forest around her. His design just fit into the trees as a part of its surroundings. She crossed to the doorway that didn't yet have a door and she entered. Of course, the interior wasn't finished but still the bones were there and she laughed with delight and awe. The stairs to the upper floor were there and she hurried across and made her way up them. She was delighted when she realized she could step into the room. The view was everything she'd dreamed it would be. Nothing but topaz and shades of teal blue as far as she could see.

"What do you think?" Trent called, drawing her attention down to where he stood on the first landing of the walkway. He grinned up at her.

"I love it!"

"Good. You look great up there. And I'm glad to finally see your smiling face."

"You are amazing. You and Jacob have worked your magic in an amazing and speedy way. How did you do this?"

"The outside goes up fast if nothing is being changed." He smiled. "Since you weren't around, there was nothing to change."

"But nothing needed to be. I love this. I can't wait to see what it looks like when you are finished."

"Hang on, I'll be right back. I need to grab something." He jogged down the steps and down the path. In minutes, he returned, carrying a paper coffee cup. "I bought you this in the hopes that I might see you today. I was starting to have a real fight on my hands not to come and bang your door down."

"So you're saying I came outside just in the nick of time."

"Oh yeah. Do you know how many times I've had to talk your brother out of coming and doing just that? He's been worried about you."

He disappeared inside the house and she lost sight of him. She was grateful that he hadn't come and disturbed her. She'd needed the time. But now she wasn't sure what she needed. Except that cup of coffee he carried.

And maybe a little Trent time.

Okay, so she'd had several moments when she'd had to stop herself from thinking about him. Trent had gotten to her and now she just had to figure out what to do about it.

"Hey." His head appeared above the landing and then he joined her. He grinned and handed her the coffee. Their fingers brushed and she immediately felt light-headed and light-kneed. *Goodness, this was ridiculous. She was not ready for this.*

"Thank you for this. You know, I was dying for

this for five days. Well, not technically for five since I've been asleep for about fifteen hours. But for a good four days, I wanted this." She'd also wanted him but she didn't dare say that. It was too scary to even contemplate.

And yet she knew it with all of her heart.

She savored her first sips of coffee. "Thank you. This is just what I needed. And it's only appropriate that I have my first cup of coffee in my treehouse with you." She raised her cup to him. "Cheers to you and what you've done here."

"It's been fun. Did you finish your book?"

"I did. And I think it's one of my best. My readers are going to like it, I believe. It's fun and romantic."

"Great."

"I'm going to see the sea turtles today. If Shar is available. And tomorrow I'm going to see Kelsey at the stables. I'm taking time off to check out my surroundings. I'm also having lunch at the resort with your sisters one day. But now that you have all this done, is it time to start picking out counters and interior styles?"

"It is. Go do your outings and maybe on Thursday we can head to the suppliers and you can start picking out what the interior will look like."

"I can't wait!"

"Good for you. Would you want to take a ride on the motorcycle tonight?"

"That would be fun."

"I'll come by about seven?"

"Sounds like a plan."

And then she jogged down the stairs and headed to her cabin and her truck. Excitement bubbled inside her. She'd known she had to put distance between them. But she hadn't been able to deny herself the motorcycle ride with Trent.

That evening, Lilly was ready when Trent rode up on his Knucklehead. She'd had a wonderful day. "Have you been there?" she asked him. "It is amazing. They rescue so many sea turtles and save them from all kinds of issues."

"I've been there. They do great work."

She hopped on the back of the motorcycle, strapped on her helmet and then wrapped her arms around Trent. They rode along the winding coast road and it felt good to feel the late afternoon sun on her skin. There were a lot of windsurfers on the water in the bay. They stopped for ice cream and then moved to a picnic table and watched the action.

"You seem more relaxed." Trent sat down beside her on the bench. He dipped his spoon into his butter pecan double dip.

"I'm getting there. I thought it was going to be so hard to start letting myself get involved but it's easier than I thought. Part of it is because I'm just loving it here so much. And the words have never come easier. And that was a shock to me."

"Why is that?"

"I'm not sure." She was trying to concentrate on the surfers and the conversation but her attention was on Trent. It had been three weeks since they'd met. She couldn't very well tell him that the hero of her last book had turned into a likeness of him and that had helped solve part of her process...the character had almost written himself after she had become inspired by Trent.

She dug into her strawberry ice cream and concentrated on the sweetness of it, forcing herself not to stare at Trent and wonder things she wasn't ready to wonder.

But she was still wondering an hour later when he dropped her off at her house. He walked her to her door like he always did and her heart clanged like cymbals when they stopped on the porch. She unlocked her door and when she turned, he was standing close to her. She inhaled the scent of him and fought the urge to wrap her arms around his neck.

"Lilly." He said her name softly and pushed her hair behind one ear. She thought for certain he was going to kiss her. Butterflies waltzed in her chest as his gaze settled on her lips but then he blinked and stepped back. "I better go. We have a busy day tomorrow."

He strode off the porch and she watched, stunned. "Are you running from me?" she asked, suddenly not in control of her voice, it seemed.

"Afraid?" He turned toward her.

"Yes." She quirked a brow at him and asked herself whether she was crazy. She was asking for trouble and her head wasn't on straight yet.

"Actually, I am." He stepped back toward her. "I already told you how I feel about you that night at my mom and dad's place. I wasn't joking. But the last thing I want to do is push you."

She was twenty-six years old and she was standing in front of a man, feeling things she'd never felt before. And she wasn't ready to back down. "What if I want you to push me?" *She was getting herself into so much trouble.* She moved toward him. "I'm cautious and scared, it's true. But Trent, I'm also…a grown woman who has met an amazing man who blurs the lines to every emotion I feel. And I can't get you off my mind."

They were nearly touching as he looked down at her. His jaw tightened and he wrapped his arms around her. "You're all I think about." And then he kissed her.

She sucked in a trembling breath just as his lips

claimed hers. Time stopped.

Then it started back up, like a kaleidoscope of colors colliding.

His heart thundered just as much as her own and then he pulled back. "That's why I haven't kissed you, Lilly. I know that once I start kissing you, I'm not going to want to stop. This isn't some test for me to see if you're ready to start dating. I've known from pretty early on that I want you. From here on out. So I don't want to scare you off but I don't want to mislead you. I lost once but I'm ready to risk everything to win your heart."

She was having trouble breathing. His kiss had flipped her world upside down. And now his words. "Oh," was all that came out of her mouth.

He smiled and gave a slight shake of his head. "Go inside, Lilly. Sleep well. We have a busy day tomorrow. We'll take this as slow as you want but I'm playing for keeps. If you decide we're going anywhere with this relationship."

And then he got on his Harley and rode away,

leaving her feeling like a knucklehead because she hadn't been able to form coherent words. And because she hadn't told him she loved him.

She couldn't. She might have just realized she loved him but she wasn't sure she could handle it.

CHAPTER TWELVE

The next week was spent picking out countertops and cabinets. Turned out Jacob and Trent were both beautiful cabinet makers and she hired them to make them. Trent set Jacob to work on them while they continued picking out fixtures and windows and so many other small items needed for a house. Though this was a treehouse, it still had all the comforts of home…just some added charm and quirks. He built her a book nook and they picked out trim for the space. Even though the majority of her sales were in eBooks, she still adored paperbacks and kept a special bunch.

She had told him this and he hadn't forgotten. They chose cedar walls and varnished floors that brought out the light marbled tones in the cedar. By the end of the week, all the choices were made and though they'd had a great time picking it all out, there had been a strain between them because he seemed almost to have moved past telling her he loved her and she wanted him to kiss her again but held her thoughts to herself.

They were unloading cedar planks when Levi called.

"Hey," Trent said. "What's up?"

Lilly saw his expression shoot to alarm. *Something was wrong.*

"I'm on my way." He hung up. "Jillian went into labor already. Levi's calling all the family. She's premature. I need to get there."

"Can I come with you?"

"Sure."

He unhooked the trailer he had carried the cedar on. Lilly jogged to the house and grabbed a sweater and her purse that she'd already set on the kitchen table. She climbed into the passenger side of the truck as he was climbing into the driver's seat. She could tell by his expression that he was worried.

"Technology is wonderful these days," she said, hoping to calm his fears and her own.

"Yes, I know. It's just Jillian had a lot of trouble conceiving. She was told she couldn't have a baby and this was a miracle. If something goes wrong…she might not get another one."

"I'm sorry, I didn't know."

"She's one of the best people I know. I don't want her to go through…"

Lilly knew what he was saying and didn't want that either. She started to pray.

He broke all the speed limits as he drove to the hospital.

By the time they reached the hospital, other family members were arriving. The waiting room quickly filled. Jake was out in the ocean somewhere on a dive and BJ was out in the ocean somewhere as a fishing guide. Shar, Olivia, and Cali were all clearly worried, and Violet and Sam too. Of course Levi, Trent, and Max were there, along with Grant and Gage. They were all worried too, their expressions tense. Lilly suddenly wondered why she'd come. She had no clue what to say to them. They all cared deeply for Jillian and Ryan and their baby girl.

This wasn't about her. It was about Jillian and the sweet life inside her.

Moments later, the doctor came out to the family with the news that it was in the best interest of the mother and child that they transport Jillian to Tampa General Hospital by helicopter where there was a neonatal intensive care unit for premature babies. Ryan would be able to ride with her.

Without hesitation, the entire waiting room moved toward the exits. Everyone jumped into vehicles and a caravan formed with Levi in the lead, escorting them through traffic, siren blaring through red lights and over the bridge onto the highway.

Lilly was tied in knots; worry shrouded her and she kept praying this would end well.

"I had time with Erica," Trent said. "Time I know was all a blessing and a gift. This is tearing me up for my sister. She needs time with her precious baby girl."

"Yes," Lilly agreed but couldn't get more out. All she could do was reach out and place her hand on his thigh. She wished she could hold his hand but it was firmly gripped on the wheel as they drove at speeds much higher than the speed limit.

The chopper had beat them there by several minutes. They all jumped from their vehicles and stormed the hospital, and searched for the neonatal unit.

"Baby April is going to be all right," Shar said, her voice firm and unrelenting for any variation of anything less than good being voiced.

They all agreed and marched toward the nurse's station. They were quickly directed to the right waiting room and the pacing began.

Trent stood by the window with his back to everyone and Lilly couldn't forget how he had stood by her the night of the party. She wanted to comfort him and went to stand beside him. She slipped her hand in his and he met her gaze.

He squeezed her hand. "Thanks."

She nodded. She so wanted to say more but just

didn't have the words. Inside, she was petrified for everyone and struggling not to show it.

Finally, the doctor came out of the double doors. The entire room went silent, not that there had been much conversation going on before.

"Mother and baby are doing good," the doctor said as he was swarmed by the family.

"Yes," Max boomed and rejoicing erupted from everyone.

The doctor grinned and continued talking, about lung development needing a little bit of help but that the baby was strong and healthy.

Lilly barely heard anything as tears streamed down her face as she looked at Trent. "The baby's okay. April's alive. Jillian's alive." She threw her arms around Trent and hugged him, burying her face in his chest. His arms tightened around her and he buried his face in her mass of hair.

"Thank God," she heard him say. Holding her, they turned to see the hugs and joyous light on everyone's faces. Olivia was beaming and on the phone; it was easy to tell that she was talking to BJ.

Jake raced into the waiting room at that moment, looking wild.

"Is she okay?" he yelled, seeing the tears before he saw the smiles.

"She's doing great, Uncle Jake," Trent called.

Jake let out a whoop and then grabbed his mom in a hug and spun her around the room. "Congratulations, Grandma!"

Little Kevin was all smiles as he raced from Levi's side, where he'd been jumping with excitement, and threw his arms around Violet. "Now you have two of us."

Violet bent down, the look of love so full on her face as she hugged Kevin. "Yes, I do. Yes, I do. How blessed I am."

Lilly was mesmerized by them. Her thoughts went to her mom and her dad. And she thought of how much they'd loved her. And how many times her mother had told her those very words. Later, as she and Trent walked outside, she looked up at him. The sky was blue and the clouds fluffy perfection. It was a glorious day in so many ways.

"Trent." She looked into his beloved face. "You're right. My parents would want me to move forward. They did feel blessed to have me and BJ and they told us so all the time. Like your mom did just now with Kevin. But I was the blessed one. Today reminded me of that."

"Me too. Life is precious. And we only have so long to be with the ones we love. Lilly, I want to be with you. I'm blessed to have found you."

She smiled and for the first time in so long, there was no weight on her shoulders. "I've found you. And I have only one wish and that's to spend the rest of my life with you. I love you, Trent Sinclair."

His smile melted her heart and then he pulled her into his arms. "I'm going to spend the rest of my life making all your wishes come true because you just made mine come true."

And then he kissed her with all the passion of every happy ending she'd ever written.

"Hey, so I'm guessing Jillian and the baby are fine and so are you two?" BJ grinned at them as they broke the kiss. "I'm a little late but looks like I got here in time for the good stuff."

Lilly laughed. "Oh yes. The very, very good stuff."

"Well, get back to it. I'm going to go get one of those celebration kisses from my beautiful wife."

"You do that." Trent chuckled and bent his head to Lilly and kissed her again.

EPILOGUE

Four weeks after sweet baby April was born the family stood on the walkway leading up to Lilly's treehouse as Lilly and Trent stood on the deck and exchanged their wedding vows. Trent had worked hard on making her dream spot a reality and she'd taken a little time off between finishing her last series and starting her new one. Lilly was enjoying the break and planned to develop a more well-rounded life when she started back up.

"So now you two have two houses, which will you live in?" Grant asked. Cali was leaning back against his chest and he had his arms around her. They looked happy together. "This is a great place you've built Trent. Very creative."

Trent had his arm over Lilly's shoulders and he kissed her temple, making her smile and feel loved. Love. Such a hard thing for her to open up to had ended up being easy with Trent. Oh how she loved him.

"We are going to base at my house and this is going to be Lilly's writing retreat. And our special getaway. If there is one thing I learned early about Lilly is that she needs her writing place and I made sure this was exactly what she wanted."

"He certainly did. It is everything I dreamed of and more." Her heart was so full of emotions she was having a hard time expressing herself. She wrapped her arms around his waist and looked up at him. "You amaze me."

He smiled. "I try. But I have a lot to live up to."

Jake looked down from where he was standing above them on the upper deck with Max and Kelsey admiring the ocean view. "And that'd be an affirmative. I think she writes about hunky heroes in her stories. Speaking of which, have you put me in one yet? I am the only available Sinclair left you know." He grinned wolfishly as Max leaned over to look down.

"Yeah, maybe add him to a story and see if you can conjure up a woman that can hold him. The guy has major commitment concerns."

Kelsey was looking down too and her smile was wide. "I think you should do that."

"Hey, I'm just teasing," Jake said, backpedaling as everyone joined in on his female issues. "I don't need anyone's help in the romance department. I'm doing just fine."

Trent laughed. "Help him if you can but the man might be uncatchable. But it's going to be fun watching when the right woman comes along and ties him in knots. He'll probably fall harder and faster than any of us have. Though I fell hard myself."

"Me too," she said as he brushed a kiss on her lips. She sighed. She'd fallen like a rock and was now flying like a rocket. She was so happy. She smiled across the way at BJ and Olivia who were cooing to and infatuated with the baby. Oliva carefully took her from Jillian who looked so content. Motherhood looked good on Jillian. And Ryan. The man was literally radiating with pride. And Sam and Violet hovered close too.

"Mom, Dad!" Kevin yelled suddenly and stuck his head over the upper railing. He'd been up in her office exploring since Trent had told him there was a surprise up there if he could find it. "There's a secret hatch up here. If you open it there's a zipline!"

Levi and Jessica were down on the ground on the flagstone area that Trent had added with seating and an outdoor grilling area, along with Cam and Lana and Shar and Gage. They all looked up at little Kevin.

"Seriously," Levi called and shot Trent a questioning look. "Tell me you didn't do that?"

"Hey, relax," Trent assured him. "It's safe. I'll strap him in it in a minute and you'll see. I wanted Lilly to have a quick way to get down if she needed it."

"But a zipline?" Jessica asked, looking a little alarmed too.

Shar was already on her way up the stairs. "Hey, I'm doing it. I think it's cool. Awesome idea, big brother."

Gage was right behind her. "I think this party just took a turn on the wild side. I want in."

Lilly was laughing now. She'd already tried out her little wedding present surprise and had given Trent an extra-long kiss for it. "I love it. I knew they would too." She shot the protective parents a glance. "Well, almost everyone."

Trent's eyes twinkled. "And I love you. And they'll see that I'm not only a great treehouse builder but a stickler for safety. Believe me, cautious police chief Levi will be loving it too after he takes his first ride. You may never get any peace up here now that they know about the zipline."

She looked around at her new family. "That's okay. I'm not a hermit hiding out anymore. And not only is my life better now, but my writing will be too. And all because you reached out and gave me your hand, your love, and your understanding when I really needed you."

"And when you took my hand you showed me the way to my future. I love you, Mrs. Sinclair."

She smiled. No, she beamed with loving him.

"Uncle Trent," Kevin called. "Would you *pul-eeze* stop kissing Aunt Lilly and let me ride this thing?"

"Hey, me too," Jake called. "You can kiss her later. We want to fly!"

Trent took her hand. "Come on, he's right. More kissing later and that's a promise. So be ready."

She laughed. "Oh, believe me, I won't be letting you forget that promise."

And then she followed him up the stairs…

Excerpt from

WITH THIS FOREVER

Windswept Bay, Book Ten

CHAPTER ONE

Jake Sinclair rammed a hand through his hair as he watched the last of the dive group headed off the dock and walk toward the back entrance of his dive shop. His eyes narrowed when the tall blonde with an attitude turned back and drilled him with fierce, angry eyes. She'd been part of a three-party group mixed in with the other seven-party group. And she'd been trouble from the moment she'd set foot on his boat.

Hoping she'd leave, he turned away and knelt

down to double-check that the boat was secured to the dock correctly. He knew it was secured just fine but checking it gave him a reason to look away and let Brandy stomp her way off the dock and off the premises.

Rapid steps on the pier told him no such luck, she was coming back. He braced himself for another unpleasant encounter and shot a glance over his shoulder. A little too late as she shoved him in the back and sent him off the pier. He splashed into the bay and hit the water on his side, did a quick flip and came up fast. A few years as a Navy SEAL, and more years as a dive master, kept him quick in the water. Obviously not as quick as he should be out of the water.

"Okay, that does it—you've got a problem, lady?" he called, spitting mad and tired of ignoring her ridiculous actions in hopes she'd just leave.

She glared down at him with her hands gripping her slender hips. "You ignored me. Nobody does that. And that's what you get. I'm the best thing that could have happened to you."

"Honey, for some reason I'm pretty sure that isn't

true."

"Don't call me honey. You lost your chance at that." She hiked her nose in the air then stormed down the pier like the Tasmanian Devil in a string bikini.

He'd done everything possible to be nice to her without taking her up on her over-the-top advances. He'd finally had to point-blank tell her that he was thirty-two years old and she was nineteen and he wasn't interested. Not to mention she was also not a nice person. And just being sexy wasn't cutting it these days for Jake.

"Come on," she snapped at her friends, who were waiting for her.

They'd obviously had enough and both shook their heads.

"That was not nice, and uncalled for," the nicest of the three, Diana, said. "I'll get my own ride back home."

Good for her. The other girl gave Diana and then him a regretful look before she followed Brandy across the lot. *At least Diana had some sense.*

He swam to the back of the boat.

"That was intense," Caleb, his dive assistant, said as Jake climbed out of the water onto the platform.

"Pretty ridiculous is what I call it." He yanked his shirt off and tossed it to the floor of the boat. "I pity the dude who gets tangled up with that one."

He did not do drama. He enjoyed dating, maybe a little too much. He enjoyed spending time with intriguing women. But nothing about Brandy had intrigued him. She'd been spoiled and mean-spirited from the moment she'd climbed onto his boat. And for some strange reason, she'd thought she could impress him with her bad-mannered moves. He'd dodged her from instant one.

It had been the longest, four-hour round-trip dive excursion he'd ever been on and he'd been thankful they hadn't paid for a five-hour trip. He would have had to call it quits and brought them in early.

Caleb chuckled. "Yeah, that was one scary chick right there."

"Tell me about it." He scowled. "Please tell me I didn't do anything to make her think I was in to her or—"

"Are you kidding?" Caleb broke him off before he could voice any more of his concern that he'd led her on somehow. "You didn't do anything. Diana said she's done this before with guys. She said Brandy spotted you at Paradise Grill one night and has been watching you."

"Watching me?" He raked a hand through his short, wet hair.

"She's got pictures of you on her phone, like she's been trailing you or something."

"Yay for me," Jake muttered. Just what he needed—a college-aged stalker. "I'm sure she's deleting those photos now. Probably burning her phone. Maybe you need to head into the shop and make sure Miss Sunshine isn't causing any trouble inside her car."

"Sure thing." Caleb glanced toward the brunette who hadn't gone with her friends.

"I might see if Diana needs a ride home."

"Yeah, she probably needs it. Tell Fran to lock up the front and I'll take care of the back."

Fran worked the shop while he and his other dive

master took the daily dive trips. Jake watched Caleb and Diana head toward the shop, then he turned back to the boat with a sense of relief. Tension eased from his shoulders as he headed into the cabin and pulled a bottle of water from the cooler. He downed the whole thing in less than thirty seconds then he went back up on deck, ready to chill out for a moment. Movement out of the corner of his eye caught his attention and he glanced toward land, half expecting to see blondezilla storming his way again. Instead, he saw a tall, dark-headed woman at the door of the vacant shop connected to his dive shop.

She was stunning, really stunning. He lost all train of thought for a moment as he took her in. She wore a flowing yellow dress that fluttered in the breeze from the bay. As he stared, she turned and caught him looking. Their eyes collided and he froze to the spot.

Who was she?

She headed toward the faded blue van backed into the parking space with its back doors open. Jake watched her load her arms with boxes. She could barely see around the armload but started back to the shop. *There was no way she could see where she was going.* He saw her veer to the left then to the right and he wanted to yell out for her to watch her step, but he didn't. He just held his breath and to his surprise, she made it inside the building without breaking her neck.

Who was she?

His landlord hadn't said anything about someone renting the shop. He would've thought Mrs. Louis would have told him if she'd decided to rent out the space.

The woman reappeared and went back to the van. When she started stacking more boxes in her arms, he decided he needed to go offer to help her. She had started back toward the building as he hopped from the boat. No sooner had he started her way than she went down like a brick wall.

He was already moving, racing down the pier to help her.

Sammy Jo Lovely yelped as she slammed to the ground and face-planted in the middle of the stack of newly sewn, custom skirts she'd been carrying. She managed to turn her hands to try to break her fall but she could tell from the stinging pain that she'd skinned a knee.

She let the impact of the fall settle over her with a groan then rolled to her back and stared up at the picturesque blue sky above her. Of course, the first thought was to wonder if anyone had witnessed her do this clumsy face-plant.

Groaning again, she struggled to sit up.

"Wait," someone yelled. "Don't move."

She looked toward the docks to see the gorgeous, shirtless guy from the boat at the pier who she'd been distracted by moments before her fall. He put both hands on the railing separating the dock from the grassy expanse between them and vaulted effortlessly over the railing and charged her way. *All muscled, tanned, overwhelming inch of him.*

She froze and just watched him cross to her. Seconds later, he knelt by her side and she was blinking at him like an owl at daybreak. Her mouth fell open and she clamped it shut.

"You're hurt. And bleeding," he said, seeing her palms. "Let me help you."

"I'm fine," she managed. Her heart raced. He was so distracting that momentarily she was feeling no pain at all.

"I hate to be the bearer of bad news, but you're not okay." His deep blue eyes were compassionate as he looked at her then her palms and then down toward her knees.

She sighed. "You might be right. I should have been watching where I was going."

"You did have your arms full." He gently helped her sit up by slipping an arm beneath her shoulders and easing her up.

"Great. I was hoping no one saw my act of graceful tumbling." It was one thing to fall flat on her face and no one see her do it. It was an altogether complete other solar system of embarrassing knowing he'd seen the whole thing. Pain was now radiating from her knee and her palms. She bit her lip and tried to ignore it.

"It doesn't matter. You're hurting."

"Just my knee mostly. I'm afraid to look." She gave a shaky laugh. "I'm kind of a chicken when it comes to blood."

"Then don't look. I'll get you inside and take care of it for you."

"No, I can make it—" Her words turned into a gasp when he stood and scooped her into his arms. "Oh, I wasn't expecting you to carry me."

"Well, I am. Do you have water in there?"

"Yes, but this is a bit awkward." Very awkward, actually, to find herself held against his very strong chest with his arms hooked under her knees and her back. She felt breathless looking into his blue, blue eyes.

He cocked his head to the side and winked at her. "I'm Jake Sinclair. I own the dive shop next door. Knowing my name hopefully makes it less awkward. Now, who are you?"

She blinked, trying to look away but could not make herself do so. "Sammy Jo Lovely, otherwise known from here on out as Miss Not-So-Graceful."

He entered the back door. "You're being too hard

on yourself. It's nice to meet you, Sammy Jo Lovely."

She gulped hard as he stared into her eyes while striding, oh so capably, across the room to the chair next to the wall. She hadn't been able to walk two feet carrying a few boxes without falling flat on her face and he was carrying her not-so-light-body, *and* staring into her eyes at the same time. She fought the urge to let her injured hands rest on his impressive, bare-naked chest.

Thankfully he made it to the chair and gently set her in it, then straightened and looked around. "Now point me in the direction of water and a clean cloth and I'll take care of your wounds."

She tried to keep her act together considering he was seemingly unaffected by her not-so-impressive charms. "In there." She pointed toward the bathroom.

He gave her a devastating smile that kicked her insides into a frenzy and she could only imagine had caused much more sophisticated women than herself to lose their hearts, and maybe their heads over him. She had just witnessed the beautiful blonde storm down the pier and shove him into the water. Maybe that had been what had happened to her. Just lost her head over the dark-haired, gorgeous man.

She'd been startled when she'd looked out at the newly arrived boat and witnessed what the woman did. And it had been easy for her to think the guy must have deserved what he'd gotten. But now, she wondered how *anyone* could be mad at him. He was amazing.

He came from the restroom carrying a damp cloth.

"You're really going above and beyond what you need to do. I can take it from here."

He knelt, took one of her hands, and gently lay the cool wet cloth against the scraped skin. "I hope I'm not the only person who would help out in a situation like this. Sorry if that burns." He took her other hand and lightly pressed it with the wet cloth between both palms. His touch was easy and sent her pulse speeding as he smiled at her. "Hold them together and let the coolness of the rag seep in. I'm going to look at your knee, if that's okay with you?"

Her granny would call him a sweetheart and she had to agree. "I hate to admit it but that would probably be best."

Very carefully, he pressed both her palms together on the cloth. "How is that?"

"It stings, but is feeling better. They aren't too bad, just a few minor scrapes. You're a very nice person. I wasn't expecting that after I saw that pretty blonde woman shove you into the water." The moment the words burst from her lips she gasped.

His eyes swung to hers and suddenly she wished with all her heart she had kept her thoughts to herself.

Why had she even said that?

More Books by Debra Clopton

Star Gazer Inn of Corpus Christi Bay
What New Beginnings are Made of (Book 1)
What Dreams are Made of (Book 2)
What Hopes are Made of (Book 3)
What a Heart's Desire is Made of (Book 4)
What True Love is Made of (Book 5)

Sunset Bay Romance
Longing for Forever (Book 1)
Longing for a Hero (Book 2)
Longing for Love (Book 3)
Longing for Ever After (Book 4)
Longing for You (Book 5)
Longing for Us (Book 6)

Texas Brides & Bachelors
Heart of a Cowboy (Book 1)
Trust of a Cowboy (Book 2)
True Love of a Cowboy (Book 3)

New Horizon Ranch Series
Her Texas Cowboy: Cliff (Book 1)
Rescued by Her Cowboy: Rafe (Book 2)
Protected by Her Cowboy: Chase (Book 3)
Loving Her Best Friend Cowboy: Ty (Book 4)
Family for a Cowboy: Dalton (Book 5)
The Mission of Her Cowboy: Treb (Book 6)
Maddie's Secret Baby (Book 7)
This Cowgirl Loves This Cowboy: Austin (Book 8)

Turner Creek Ranch Series
Treasure Me, Cowboy (Book 1)
Rescue Me, Cowboy (Book 2)
Complete Me, Cowboy (Book 3)
Sweet Talk Me, Cowboy (Book 4)

Cowboys of Ransom Creek
Her Cowboy Hero (Book 1)
The Cowboy's Bride for Hire (Book 2)
Cooper: Charmed by the Cowboy (Book 3)
Shane: The Cowboy's Junk-Store Princess (Book 4)
Vance: Her Second-Chance Cowboy (Book 5)
Drake: The Cowboy and Maisy Love (Book 6)
Brice: Not Quite Looking for a Family (Book 7)

Texas Matchmaker Series
Dream With Me, Cowboy (Book 1)
Be My Love, Cowboy (Book 2)
This Heart's Yours, Cowboy (Book 3)
Hold Me, Cowboy (Book 4)
Be Mine, Cowboy (Book 5)
Operation: Married by Christmas (Book 6)
Cherish Me, Cowboy (Book 7)
Surprise Me, Cowboy (Book 8)
Serenade Me, Cowboy (Book 9)
Return To Me, Cowboy (Book 10)
Love Me, Cowboy (Book 11)
Ride With Me, Cowboy (Book 12)
Dance With Me, Cowboy (Book 13)

Windswept Bay Series
From This Moment On (Book 1)
Somewhere With You (Book 2)
With This Kiss (Book 3)
Forever and For Always (Book 4)
Holding Out For Love (Book 5)
With This Ring (Book 6)
With This Promise (Book 7)
With This Pledge (Book 8)
With This Wish (Book 9)
With This Forever (Book 10)
With This Vow (Book 11)

About the Author

Bestselling author Debra Clopton has sold over 2.5 million books. Her book OPERATION: MARRIED BY CHRISTMAS has been optioned for an ABC Family Movie. Debra is known for her contemporary, western romances, Texas cowboys and feisty heroines. Sweet romance and humor are always intertwined to make readers smile. A sixth generation Texan she lives with her husband on a ranch deep in the heart of Texas. She loves being contacted by readers.

Visit Debra's website at www.debraclopton.com

Sign up for Debra's newsletter at
www.debraclopton.com/contest/

Check out her Facebook at
www.facebook.com/debra.clopton.5

Follow her on Twitter at @debraclopton

Contact her at debraclopton@ymail.com

If you enjoyed reading *With This Wish* I would appreciate it if you would help others enjoy this book, too.

Recommend it. Please help other readers find this book by recommending it to friends, reader's groups and discussion boards.

Review it. Please tell other readers why you liked this book by reviewing it on the retail site you purchased it from or Goodreads. If you do write a review, please send an email to debraclopton@ymail.com so I can thank you with a personal email. Or visit me at: www.debraclopton.com.